KU-732-067

THE MIDWIFE'S
NEW-FOUND
FAMILY

BY
FIONA McARTHUR

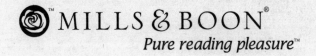

® MILLS & BOON®
Pure reading pleasure™

First published in Great Britain 2009
Harlequin Mills & Boon Limited,
Eton House, 18-24 Paradise Road, Richmond, Surrey TW9 1SR

© Fiona McArthur 2009

ISBN: 978 0 263 86843 2

Set in Times Roman 10½ on 13¼ pt
03-0509-41190

Printed and bound in Spain
by Litografía Rosés, S.A., Barcelona

Suddenly she felt at ease with this man whose life had hung so precariously this very afternoon, and with the heat of his skin against hers came the reinforcement of his survival. The satisfaction grew that this Ben was here, safe and solidly warm against her, and the other world outside the house seemed a million miles away.

He turned and dropped a gentle kiss, warm and fleeting, on her lips. It was over before she could begin to avoid it—unlike the impact. Her lips seemed to vibrate with the memory, and she mashed them together as if to blot the imprint out, because the thrumming continued in decreasing waves.

She felt suspended in time and his voice floated over her. 'Thank you for saving my life, Misty.' She could do nothing but stare back at him. His eyes were as blue as the sea he'd come from, and his gaze roamed her face at will. She could feel the heat beneath her skin under his scrutiny, and suddenly there was a clawing tumble of unbidden thoughts.

Fiona McArthur brings you a fabulous new trilogy…

LYREBIRD LAKE
MATERNITY

Every day brings a miracle…

It's time for these midwives
to become mothers themselves!

Previously we met single mum Montana Browne in…

THE MIDWIFE'S LITTLE MIRACLE

Now meet Misty Buchanan in…

THE MIDWIFE'S NEW-FOUND FAMILY

Lyrebird Lake is famous for bringing people together.
Single dad doctor Ben is ready to claim Misty
as his own—she'll be the perfect mother and bride!

Look out for Mia's story,
coming soon in Medical™ Romance

A mother to five sons, **Fiona McArthur** is an Australian midwife who loves to write. Medical™ Romance gives Fiona the scope to write about all the wonderful aspects of adventure, romance, medicine and midwifery that she feels so passionate about—as well as an excuse to travel! Now that her boys are older, Fiona and her husband Ian are off to meet new people, see new places, and have wonderful adventures. Fiona's website is at www.fionamcarthur.com

Recent titles by the same author:

THE MIDWIFE'S LITTLE MIRACLE
  Lyrebird Lake Maternity
THE MIDWIFE'S BABY
THEIR SPECIAL-CARE BABY
THE SURGEON'S SPECIAL GIFT
THE DOCTOR'S SURPRISE BRIDE

To midwives and mothers everywhere.
You continue to inspire me.

CHAPTER ONE

Out of the mist she saw a man and a circle of shells.

Misty Buchanan knew it was the future and not a dream because she'd come to recognise the difference over the years. She hadn't expected a premonition while beach fishing on this deserted coastline because she'd been so caught up in the pleasure of the salty breeze in her face.

Her sight shimmered and dimmed and she accepted she had no choice but to watch as she closed her eyes…

He balanced on a jumbled spit of rocks beside some seagulls, and even in the haze of time his torso looked spectacular against the backdrop of the ocean as he cradled the bird against him to unwind the twine. She couldn't see his face but there was something about his concern for the tangled gull that felt familiar on a different level.

When Misty had been younger it had frightened her to see people and situations with such clarity with her eyes shut, but now she accepted it as part of her life, albeit a small part, for only rarely did the future affect her present.

Though this gift brought responsibility with it and her heart thumped with the double-edged sword of what could be revealed.

The bird in his hand was suddenly free and he stepped back out of the way.

Misty frowned as she lost the sight and then the mists cleared again. She drew her breath in sharply.

His head smashed against the rocks as he fell and then his body rolled into a green wave to float without direction away from the rocks.

The vision dissipated and she knew it was useless to attempt to retrieve it. She had been shown all she would be.

Misty spun and her fingers clenched on her beach rod and bucket as she raced towards her Jeep. Once there she tossed them into the back haphazardly as her gaze scanned the distance for clues.

The Southern Queensland beach stretched for miles both ways and each ended with a rocky outcrop into the ocean.

In the distance a flock of gulls soared above a tall white lighthouse that overlooked the water like a guardian.

The visions never came without the opportunity to somehow influence the course of events so she'd have to trust to instinct as she slewed the vehicle with reckless speed through the sand towards the lighthouse.

Misty's vehicle slid to a halt and she threw open her door. She grabbed the boogie board she kept for belly surfing and the hot sand squeaked in protest as she tore across the beach and onto the grainy boulders of the outcrop. All she could do was pray this was the correct headland.

Her stomach plummeted as she gazed into the choppy green water between the swells. Nothing. It had to be the wrong headland!

As she turned to race back to the car her final glance caught the roll of a long brown arm and then she saw his lifeless body as he slid face down along the back of a wave.

'Help,' she muttered unhappily as she looked at the rocks that broke the swells as they drove in.

'Big breath,' she encouraged herself out loud, then scrambled inelegantly to the water's edge and dived into the next wave with the board under her. Her breath sucked in as the cold water splashed around her and dormant resuscitation drills pounded into her mind as she paddled furiously towards her target.

The occasional swell washed over her face and she spat out salty water as she tried to calculate how long he would have been unconscious.

That first touch when she grasped his arm gave her a rush of relief that at least she'd made it out to him. His skin was warm even in the water and she heaved his arm and shoulder over until he rolled half over the board and she could tread water beside him. By default his head rose from the water. She sank below the surface to push his other armpit onto the boogie board and his weight came off her so she could rest.

'Hello. Wake up. Open your eyes.' But there was no response when she shook his arm. Twice she blew into his cold lips and twice he didn't respond.

Another wave washed over both of them, She needed to get him to shore. 'Stay with me, friend,' she urged into his ear as she dragged the board around to face the beach. She steered him sideways away from the rocks as the desperate urgency of his condition propelled her through the water faster than she would have dreamed possible.

Twice more she blew into his mouth between swells and then a larger swell closed in on them and she angled the board so that they were lifted swiftly towards the beach. Another big swell carried them until a sudden wave swept them forward and tumbled them in an ungainly pile in the shallow water. She spat out seawater as she twisted on her side to hang onto him.

The wave that had been powerful enough to throw them there seemed intent on proving it could pull them back. He began to slip and she knew she didn't have the strength to return to the water after him.

'Come on,' she gritted out between her teeth, and she yanked him towards her with a desperate heave and he slid across the sand. The wave receded and it was then she noticed the tiny rivulets of his blood that went with it.

Her heart pounded noisily in her ears as she dragged in welcome air before she rolled him over and pulled him an extra foot away from the reach of the next wave.

His eyes were open, blue like his lips, and his white face was as unmoving as his chest as the water drained away from around him.

It was too late!

She bent to lay her ear against his battered chest. Thump… Thump… Thump… She could hear it. He had a heartbeat. It was slow, less than forty beats a minute probably, but so much better than no heart-beat at all.

She pushed him until he rolled onto his side and water trickled from his mouth, but he didn't move.

She shook him and he rolled back onto his back. 'Hey. Wake up, you!' Misty tilted his head and after a quick glance to check his airway was clear she breathed another two quick breaths into his lungs as she watched his chest rise. Yes. Out of the water now she could tell there was chest movement.

She pushed rhythmically on the lower third of his sternum to compress his ribcage and prayed cardiac massage would speed his sluggish heart. Thirty quick depressions, then Misty pinched his nose and blew into his mouth again.

After several desperate cycles he twitched and finally stirred, his chest moved of its own volition, and he gurgled a bubbling stream of sea water as he instinctively rolled onto his side.

Misty sat back and drew deep panting breaths of her own as the stranger coughed and wheezed his way to life.

Her shoulders began to shake in earnest and she wrapped her arms around her chest in comfort as she stared down at him. Hot tears trickled unchecked down her cheeks along with a strangled sob of mixed euphoria and horror. She sucked in a big breath to calm herself and squeezed her arms around her body harder.

Focus. Don't fall to pieces yet. She could hardly believe it.

He was alive.

She glanced out at the ocean in incredulity and her pretty pink boogie board bobbed merrily in the swells as it drifted out to sea.

She'd done it.

She glanced down at the broken strap on her wrist and strained to remember when it had sheared.

Who cared? Someone would enjoy the board.

Ben Moore hovered in a beam of light and stared down at his body as it floated in the water. He dreamed in flashes that defined his life.

Each flash contained an ocean of memories. His daughter's birth, his wife's death, a patient's family hugging him, a baby's first breath, a mermaid with long auburn hair and green eyes holding out her hand.

He smiled at her beauty. He was definitely dying. Something jolted him and he felt himself fall.

The other pictures faded away until only her vivid emerald eyes remained, and they came closer as she kissed him. Then he was coughing and retching and reality crashed in on him along with the fire in his lungs and the pain in his pounding head.

When the fit settled he took another tearing breath and hoped to avoid the painful mix of seawater and air, but it was not to be. When that convulsion died down he eased his shoulders from the gritty sand on which he was lying and ran his hands over his lacerated chest.

The surging waves lapped his feet and above him knelt the mermaid in person—except she had the most beautiful thighs in tattered denim shorts and long gorgeous legs—definitely not a mermaid, he thought fuzzily.

He glanced at her fine boned arms and the slender frame that was clearly outlined in the singlet top plastered to her skin. How on earth had she dragged him above the level of the waves?

As if she knew what he was thinking her voice washed over him, warm and reassuring, and the fact that he could hear the sound from her lips meant he really had survived.

'We rode a wave in and I pulled you the rest of the way,' she said. 'You've hit your head and torn your skin on the rocks.'

Her long red hair was tied in a limp ponytail that dripped silver rivulets of seawater between her breasts and she flipped it over to her back, which helped the thin singlet to plaster itself to her breasts even more.

He sucked his breath in with disastrous results and, when that spasm passed, the air in his lungs finally began to feel less like lava and more like the cooler gravel he needed to survive. 'Thank you.' His cracked words finally emerged.

He inhaled gingerly again. 'What happened?' Amazing how much energy just a few words took.

'Don't talk yet.' She winced at his obvious discomfort and her hand slid down over his wrist, smooth and cool and very practised as she palpated his pulse. 'I guess you fell into the water and hit your head. You nearly drowned.'

She was looking at him as if he might not understand but he understood all right. She'd saved his life and put her own very much at risk to do it.

He just couldn't think of anything to say at that moment.

She went on and he closed his eyes as he listened to her talk more to herself than to him. 'I need to get you to a hospital for observation. Salt water can cause delayed pulmonary oedema in your lungs.'

He'd have to move or she'd think he couldn't and he didn't want her having to spend more energy than she already had on him. He eased himself into a sitting position but even that hurt.

Ben rocked his head gently and couldn't help the tiny groan that escaped at the pain from his skull. It hurt like hell but he didn't need a hospital. He needed his bed.

'Thank you.' He paused for breath. 'Just my shack.' He paused again. 'I'll be fine.'

He watched her roll her eyes and it amused him in a ridiculous, semi-hysterical way. No doubt it was the euphoria of having been snatched from the jaws of death.

'You need a good check-up,' she said. 'Does your head swim?'

He put his hand up for her to grasp so he could stand. 'Better than my body does when I'm knocked out, apparently.'

'A joker,' she muttered. 'Just what I need.' Misty took his hand and shared his weight as he rose, but still he swayed against her before he could steady himself, and she knew he was hanging on to his balance by sheer willpower.

The feel of his strong hand left hers bizarrely energised and she looked down at his fingers curled around her own. She frowned at the strangeness of a connection that shouldn't even have registered then shrugged the thought away. At this moment she needed to help him stagger to her vehicle and that was enough to contend with.

When at last she had him there she didn't like the

way his head lolled against the seat as if he could barely support its weight.

'You OK?' she asked as she reached across and buckled his seat belt.

He mumbled something she didn't catch and Misty stared anxiously into his shadowed face as she leaned back into her own seat. The strong line of his jaw and angled cheeks were softened by the fact he hadn't shaved that day. Funny how that darkened stubble in no way detracted from his rugged good looks. He'd become even more attractive with the passing of time. Even more attractive? Ouch! Mind on job, she admonished herself silently.

That was if he survived. 'Hello? Wake up.' She rested her hand on his damp shoulder. 'I need directions if you want me to take you home.'

She was definitely having second thoughts about leaving him alone in a beach house to die. If he started to look worse than he did now she'd ring her brother at Lyrebird Lake and ask what to do, even though Andy's hospital was hours away, his advice would help.

'I'm sorry.' He didn't open his eyes but his apology emerged clearly this time and she felt the building tension ease from the tautness in her neck.

He paused as if it hurt to talk, and she realised it probably did.

'Name's Ben Moore. My beach house.' He paused again. 'There's a side road past the camping ground on the left.' Without opening his eyes, he said, 'You can drive around the gate instead of opening it.' He coughed again. 'The shack's about two kilometres along.'

Benmore. 'Like the beautiful gardens in Scotland?' She asked absently as she steered the vehicle across the sand. He didn't answer.

Misty concentrated on navigating the thick sand of the track onto the road and even then her four-wheel-drive slewed sideways over the mounds made by other off-road vehicles.

Once she hit the hard dirt the noise from the tyres reverberated through the cab. She'd have to remember to fill them with air when she passed the next gas station but the deflation had made a huge difference in the soft sand.

She turned her Jeep left at the campsite, spotted the entrance he'd mentioned, and drove around the locked gate onto another dirt road. She'd had no idea the track was there and it wound through the seaside scrub parallel to the beach until they climbed a grass-covered knoll.

On top and surrounded by smaller sand dunes stood a solid beach house made of sand-coloured wood. Because of the height of the knoll it over-looked the beach in both directions and tufts of coarse beach grass and wind-bent coastal shrubs ringed it.

The house was sturdily built on stilts and a lot larger than Misty's idea of a shack. A wide, shaded veranda looked out over the vista below and she parked the car in the shade beside a late model Range Rover and some steep steps.

Ben's eyes were still shut and she touched his arm. 'Will you be able to get inside, Ben?'

'I'm fine,' he said, and his eyes opened slowly to reveal the aqua irises she'd only glimpsed at the beach. His next words made her smile.

'You OK?' His concern was sweet but unfortunately the brightness of his eyes made his pale cheeks even more concerning.

'I'll be better when you have a bit of colour in your face.' She shivered and the memory of him floating face down in the water hit her. How she'd almost been unable to hold him before the wave dragged them back made her shake her head.

She recalled those vital few seconds when he'd not been breathing and she'd urged him to wake up, and then he'd moved and coughed as he returned to life.

She still couldn't believe she'd managed it. This flesh-and-blood, breathing human being would be dead if she hadn't been there. That thought left her with a deep nausea that rose out of nowhere and couldn't be denied.

'Excuse me,' she gulped, and wrenched open her door to throw herself on the ground where at least she was out of sight to be ingloriously sick.

'I'm sorry.' Soft words full of self-reproach floated around her as Ben appeared beside her, He scooped her ponytail from her face and held it behind her head while she completed the job. For the moment she was too unwell to care.

'Poor brave mermaid,' he said soothingly, and his warm hand cupped her forehead in comfort. She could feel the prick of tears in her eyes as the nausea passed. She wasn't brave. She'd been terrified.

'I'm sorry.' She allowed him to help her to her feet and then she backed away from him as she wiped her mouth with the back of her hand and schooled any expression from her face. Weakness in front of this man made her feel like a self-conscious teenager and she was supposed to be in charge.

She banished any thought of what had just happened and changed the subject. 'I'm supposed to be nursing you.'

'I'm fine.' When she didn't look convinced he shrugged and gestured wearily to the stairs. 'You can check me out now you're feeling better.'

She could see he'd shifted his concern from himself to her and she felt the undeniable pull that shimmered around Ben as if her heart was telling her something her head had to disbelieve.

'Come with me,' he said, and the cadence, those simple words, caught her heart as his long fingers caught her other hand.

There it was. That recognition she'd noticed before. It was as if his whole arm pulled her along not so much by his strength but by magnetic attraction between them that shouldn't be there.

Weakly, with her inner voice quietly insisting she leave, she followed him up the steps and into his house. She'd just see that he was OK.

CHAPTER TWO

INSIDE the house dark lacquered wood floors show-cased several glowing rugs that screamed of ancient Persia and threw glorious splashes of colour against the darkness. Bizarrely, she felt strangely at home.

Odd-shaped chairs constructed from driftwood stood around the walls and a huge, ancient seaman's chest used as a table was covered with books.

The glassed circular centre of the house had three other rooms leading off it. Ben drew her into a sunlit bathroom furnished like a shiny capsule from a luxury motor yacht complete with a huge round tub on one side that looked over the beach, then he finally let her go.

She looked down at her hand, and incredibly her fingers looked normal. So why did they pulse with the sensation of being held by this man? She'd expected her skin where he'd touched to at least glow.

No such fanciful complaint seemed to bother him as he passed her a fresh facecloth and towel.

'There's a new toothbrush in the drawer. I'll leave you to it.' Then he closed the door behind him as he left.

She stared into the oval mirror that someone had surrounded incongruously with a circle of inexpertly glued shells. Were these the shells from the vision? Her pale and strained face stared back at her. So she was meant to be here?

OK. So she'd made a fool out of herself by throwing up. But it wasn't every day you came across a man face down in the water.

She tried not to think of what would have happened if she hadn't had the premonition, but she would never again even hint that she regretted the oddness of her occasional second sight.

That gift had saved this man's life, and she would be forever grateful.

The cold water helped restore normality as it splashed against her heated cheeks, and as she brushed her teeth Misty glanced once more at her reflection.

A little colour had crept back into her face and she couldn't subdue the tiny flutter of ridiculous satisfaction that all the years of her nurse's training had stood by her on the beach.

She'd saved a life.

Here she stood, alone with a handsome stranger in his beach house, and she couldn't deny there was a delectable magnetism about the man that had her intrigued.

As long as she remembered this was a moment out of time and not the real world.

When she opened the bathroom door the central room proved empty, and as she glanced around the worry returned that maybe Ben wasn't as well as he'd seemed a few minutes ago.

'In here.' His voice sounded infinitely fatigued and her step quickened.

Ben sat on the edge of a wide white bed with a towel around his waist. She pulled her eyes and thoughts back from considering what lay underneath that towel—what on earth was she thinking?—and looked at his face.

The profile she recognised from the vision now seemed indelible in her mind. His chest showed lines of angry abrasions and her sensible side returned as she crossed the room quickly.

She sank to her knees beside the bed in front of him and looked up into his face. She examined his eyes as well as she could in the dim room. Both pupils seemed equal and reactive when she shaded the light.

'How is your head?' She ran her fingers lightly over the spongy swelling under his hairline and he winced.

'Ouch,' she said in sympathy, but didn't pause as she continued her check. He'd have to put up with the discomfort because she needed to know if there was something worse to find.

'I can tell you're in the medical profession,' he murmured.

She grinned and palpated his scalp to ensure the bone didn't feel displaced underneath. The bump seemed slightly smaller already than when she'd first checked it.

Her hand slid around the base of his skull to check for further injury and his ink-black hair felt soft and springy, and curled around her fingers as if welcoming her touch. It seemed so long since she'd done that, she'd forgotten the sensation of running her fingers through a man's hair.

'It seems OK,' she said as she forced her fingers to untangle themselves from a warm and welcoming place they didn't want to leave.

'My head is improving all the time, especially when you stroke it.' His voice held a whisper of weary teasing and her hand bounced away as if scalded.

When she met his eyes he smiled wryly at her reaction. 'I'm sure I'll be fine. I'm cold and headachy. But I am curious to know your name.'

'Misty.' She nodded at his chest and looked at him for tacit permission before she touched it. The jagged scratches were red and welted but she couldn't see any pieces of shell in the wound. She rested her hand over the wounds and felt the heat of inflammation.

'Look at your poor chest.' A sudden mad impulse to kiss her fingertips and pat his wounds better made her straighten away from him. What on earth was the matter with her? This man was an unknown entity and after today she'd never meet him again. She glanced at the blood on her fingers and admonished herself.

She stood and nodded towards the en suite she could see across the room. 'May I use that?'

'Of course. And there's antibiotic powder on the shelf we could use.'

After washing her hands, she used a small clean towel to blot the blood from his chest and then puffed the powder onto his wounds. She stood back and tried to think what else she could do for him, but her mind was suddenly blank so she returned the towel and the powder to the tiny bathroom. When she returned at least she'd thought of something. 'Is your tetanus booster up to date?'

'Yes,' he said quietly, 'and scratches are a small price to pay.' He patted the bed next to him.

Seconds later Misty found herself sitting hip to hip with him and she had no idea how she'd got there as he slipped his arm around her shoulders and pulled her closer in mutual comfort. They sat there side by side, contemplating his lucky escape.

It did seemed weirdly appropriate to hold each other at the memory of the event and surprisingly she drew the comfort he had intended from the gesture.

Suddenly she felt at ease with this man whose life had hung so precariously in the balance that very afternoon, and with the heat of his skin against hers came the reinforcement of the knowledge of his survival. The satisfaction grew that this man was here safe and solidly warm against her, and the other world outside the house seemed a million miles away.

He turned and dropped a gentle kiss, warm and fleeting, on her lips, and it was over before she could begin to avoid it, unlike the impact. Her lips seemed to vibrate with the memory and she mashed them together as if to blot the imprint out because the thrumming continued in decreasing waves.

She felt suspended in time and his voice floated over her. 'Thank you for saving my life, Misty.' She could do nothing but stare back at him. His eyes were as blue as the ocean he'd come from and his gaze roamed her face. She could feel heat beneath her skin under his scrutiny and suddenly there was a clawing tumble of unbidden sensations in her belly.

She blinked and broke eye contact as she looked away. 'Let me see your back.'

Ben closed his eyes and twisted his body so she could see.

He sighed. At least one of them had their feet firmly on the ground. Perhaps it was his concussion but he was having difficulty concentrating on anything else but her beautiful mouth and luscious body pressed against his. This was a damn inappropriate time to start dreaming about what she would look like with her shirt off.

Then she touched his back with those slender mermaid's fingers of hers, and not being able to see her hands on him made it more erotic than it should have been. He could imagine her leaving luminous trails on his skin, like lines in the water at night.

He shifted uncomfortably as desire stirred beneath the towel and he turned and reached across to capture her hand to still her fingers.

He looked down at her hand. Such long fingers as they lay in his. Such invisible strength within them. She must have a heart as strong as a lioness's. He had no doubt that was her secret.

There was something pure and golden and un-selfish about Misty that shone so brightly even someone as jaded as he could see her worth.

His grip tightened and unconsciously he inched her back to face him until their sides touched again. And then he froze. What was he doing?

His head ached, his chest hurt and he'd nearly died. And he owed his survival to this woman.

All the more reason to act on the moment, his inner demon suggested unhelpfully.

He did not need another complication in his life and from the little he'd seen of her he had no doubt this woman could be extremely complicating.

There seemed a certain naiveté about her that warned him he was the much more experienced of the two of them, but it also unmanned him.

'Thank you, Misty. I think you'd better go.'

Her eyes widened and he saw the moment she realised what he meant. Heat dusted her cheeks and she stood up quickly and looked around the room as if she'd forgotten where the exit was.

He smiled at her disorientation even as it showed him more than anything that he'd done the right thing. So she could feel it too, he thought.

He stood to follow her to the door when without warning the room tilted away from him like the deck of a ship.

A rush of cold doused him and then nothing as he fell backwards.

Misty managed to reach out and guide him sideways and back onto the bed, but even lifting his muscled legs reminded her of the struggle she'd had to get him out of the water.

She bent to lift his lids but his eyes flickered open again and he blinked groggily as he tried to sit up.

His face shone like alabaster even in the dim room. 'What happened?'

'You fainted. I think you should stay down, Ben. I'll call an ambulance so they can check you out at the hospital.'

He lifted his hand and rested it over his eyes. 'I don't need a hospital. It would be a wasted trip for emergency services when they could be saving someone else.'

Misty stilled. 'That's ridiculous.' She ticked off his symptoms on her fingers. 'You've lost consciousness twice from a head injury, had a respiratory arrest, and are probably brewing pneumonia. You need to be observed.'

Ben rubbed his forehead. 'I'm fine. I just need to sleep.'

Misty couldn't help her hands going to her hips and she stood over him and glared. The man was exasperating. 'You might never wake up.'

He didn't look like he cared and she felt the sting of tears behind her eyes. 'Imagine the waste of energy today for me.'

Ben sighed. 'I'm sorry, Misty. You're a darling. But I'm not going anywhere. Especially to a hospital!' Finality rang in the last four words.

Misty stamped her foot and he winced at the noise. Then she felt guilty. Her voice dropped to nurse-speak. 'Come on, Ben. Be sensible. I can't just leave you.'

He sighed. 'So observe me for another hour, or the four required, and then when you feel satisfied you can go. Or stay in a spare room and leave in the morning.'

Misty glanced at her watch. Four hours. It would be dark by the time she left but what choice did she have? She did *not* want to read in the paper about a man found dead in his beach house.

She could stay until she was sure he was fine. She wasn't expected until tomorrow and would at least know he was going to be OK before she departed. She looked around but there wasn't a chair in the room, which left only the bed. She'd drag in a chair from somewhere.

Ben had moved while she'd been going over her

options. 'So how did you stumble across me in my hour of need? The beach is usually deserted.'

Misty rarely spoke about her gift and she hesitated at sharing such a personal subject with a stranger. Now was not the time to get into a discussion that would probably end with Ben thinking her fanciful.

'Just luck. I'll get a chair.'

Ben lifted his arm and pulled a pillow across from the pile at the top of the bed and put it by his side. His weary eyes twinkled despite his exhaustion.

'Here. Lie down next to me. I'll put a wall up so I don't attack you.'

'I don't think so,' Misty said, and went to explore the house to find a seat. There was a huge old recliner in the next room that looked incredibly comfortable but it would never fit through the door into Ben's room.

Then there were the driftwood chairs on the verandah that looked fabulous but when she sat on them they were like bony park benches with knobs and bends in uncomfortable places. She couldn't lounge on them for four hours.

The kitchen had high-backed bar stools and she sighed as she carried one through.

'That looks comfortable,' Ben said conversationally, but then he shook his head. 'I'll get up. I can't stand the thought of you perched up there just because you're a good Samaritan. It's really not been a good day for good Samaritans all round. I wouldn't have nearly drowned if I hadn't been trying to save a bird. It's a step too far for you to suffer further on my account.'

He was either incredibly well mannered or incredibly sneaky but she really had no choice if he threatened to get up.

'For goodness' sake, I'll lie down next to you. But don't blame me if I go to sleep. I've been driving since early this morning and spent a couple of hours in the sun this afternoon.'

'Perfect. We'll both sleep.' He closed his eyes briefly, as if they stung.

She was glad to see his eyelids droop but then he began to speak again.

'My luck must have changed,' he said with his eyes still shut. Then they opened and he said quite seriously, 'You have a way of making me forget all reason in the most disconcerting way.'

She wasn't quite sure what to do with that statement because it came just as she lowered herself onto the bed as far away as possible from him.

He smiled across at her, and it changed him into a much younger man, a less world-weary one, and for a moment her knees trembled and she was pathetically grateful she was lying and not standing because she might have collapsed, boneless, on top of him.

Then he looked away and she managed to draw a discreet steadying breath and edge an inch further away from him.

He wasn't having that. He lifted his shoulder and

slid across the bed until their shoulders were touching, and then slid his arm under and around her shoulders. Ben's hand was cool against her but insidiously heat rose up her body like black ink soaking into white chalk.

And once there the heat wasn't going anywhere. It just got warmer and warmer.

'So where have you driven from today and where are you going?'

Misty tried to focus on what he'd said. Anything to move her mind away from the slow combustion going on inside her.

Focus on the real world. That's a novel idea, she mocked herself, and organised her thoughts to where they should be.

'I'm moving to Lyrebird Lake to work in a birth centre with my brother and sister-in-law.'

Ben's interest seemed genuine. 'What does your brother do?'

'Andy? He's the GP running the bush hospital, but doesn't have much to do with the birthing side. He married my best friend and they're expecting a new baby. The unit's for women-centred care. The absolute best place to have a baby.'

He frowned, and Misty could see he was unfamiliar with the term. 'Women-centred care. Define that?'

This was a wonderful diversion from the heat in her stomach. Misty could talk about this gladly. 'Each midwife has her own caseload of clients in order to better meet the needs of the woman. It gives more satisfaction all round.' She couldn't help the excitement even she could hear in her voice.

'The idea is to give each woman holistic care that can cover all the facets of being pregnant from antenatal education, mental status, breastfeeding and, of course, caring for baby when he or she comes home.'

Ben stared at her as if he didn't get it. 'I know obstetrics but it sounds like nothing I've ever had contact with.' His voice held an extra dimension she couldn't quite place but he went on quickly as if speeding away from the topic he'd started and now regretted.

His voice dropped. 'Babies. New life.'

Ben turned his head to stare at the ceiling. 'I wonder if what happened today means my slate is clean? Can I begin a new life because I so nearly lost the old one?'

The nuance of despair could have been imagined but something in his profile tugged at Misty.

She memorised the contours of his face for the time soon when she'd have to leave. 'I believe anyone can start a new life if they are determined.'

He turned to look at her and there was a glow in his eyes that made her catch her breath. 'Maybe *you* are destined to change my life.'

Impossible dream. She lifted her hand and peered at her watch as if to remind herself she needed to leave. Not that the fish would mind if she never went back to the beach to catch them. 'I'm planning on doing a bit more with my life than running around dragging you out of life-threatening situations, Ben.'

His arms tightened. Even his aura seemed to drift around her like the sea that had almost claimed him. 'But you saved my life so beautifully,' he said.

The memories rushed back and she shivered. 'Don't joke about it, Ben, please. Today was very close.'

He stilled and then squeezed her shoulder in comfort and regret for upsetting her again. 'Resuscitation is always frightening. I'm sorry you had to do that, Misty.'

She forced her mind away from those indelible pictures and closed the subject with finality. 'I think I'll get up.'

He ignored her statement and tightened his arm around her and lowered his voice so she'd have to strain to hear him. 'So you're a midwife. That would explain the mothering you've been doing.'

Her neck ached from the strain of wanting to sink into his arm and she gave up. She rested her head back and stared rigidly at the ceiling.

She blinked. He had stars glued in constellations on the roof. It was amazing, and she imagined they would glow fabulously at night. It would have taken days to create. She frowned. He had too much time on his hands, she thought as she tried to remember what he'd said while she tried to identify the star signs. Oh, yes, midwives and mothering.

'Known a few midwives, have you?' she said.

He gave a short mirthless laugh and she was jolted out of her contemplation of his ceiling.

'In my time.' His voice held self-contempt and she frowned at the disruption to the ambience in the room.

'I worked in that environment but nothing like you've spoken about,' he said. 'It was in another lifetime and I don't think I could ever go back to that.'

'You're an obstetrician, then?' That would explain his midwife comment.

'Was.'

She let the word lie between them because something told her she'd been privileged to hear even that information. It seemed she'd done the right thing because he went on as if the words were forced out of him.

'Never going back.'

She couldn't help it. 'Why?'

He breathed deeply. 'In our job, sad things occasionally happen and everyone has bad runs. It's funny how something you would normally accept as a tragedy of nature can overwhelm you unexpectedly. That's all.'

Misty had seen her fair share of sadness but, then, she'd always felt that dealing with loss in midwifery was a privilege to share with the parents. 'I guess it depends on your own life experience how things can affect you.'

'You don't know how true that is,' he said, and the way the words dragged out of him she decided she wouldn't offer any more comments in case she caused more damage.

The silence stretched and Misty didn't know whether to change the subject or just wait. After what seemed like an eternity she eased her fingers into his palm and wrapped her hand around his to at least let him know she was aware of his pain.

At her tentative offer of comfort his fingers stiffened in surprise and then, very slowly, his fingers relaxed in hers. She was glad he hadn't rebuffed her. She sensed he wasn't used to people offering him comfort and it made her want to pull his head down onto her chest and say it was all OK. But she couldn't do that. She didn't even know this man.

Ben raised his head and laughed softly if somewhat sardonically at his hand in Misty's. 'Imagine you wanting to comfort me.'

'I don't find that amusing,' Misty said quietly.

He turned his head and looked at her. His smile softened. 'No, you wouldn't. Because you, dear Misty, are a real person, and I haven't seen your like for a very long time.'

She let go of his hand. 'Probably because you live in a beach house on a deserted beach,' she said dryly. 'You haven't seen any people. You should get out more.'

'Actually, I've done all I need to do with my life. I've written a text on postnatal depression and achieved all I was going to achieve. You should probably have left me to drown.'

Misty felt his words like a vicious jab to the stomach and she drew in a breath. 'Don't ever speak like that again,' she said fiercely.

She leaned up on one elbow and stared down into his face and glared ferociously, suddenly livid with him. He looked world-wearily amused but she didn't care. This was important.

'Every life is precious. It is sad not all patients can be saved—but you have been! By me, and that gives me some rights to tell you so. There is a desperate need for skills like yours out in this world. How dare you just fritter them away like a wastrel in your beach house?'

She barely drew breath she was so angry. 'You were given a new chance on life today, a chance you nearly didn't have. One of the mysteries of the universe is how I found you.' She poked him in the chest. 'I could have drowned trying to save you so don't you even think of letting me down.'

Misty subsided but she could feel her heart pounding with the agitation of her emotions. She didn't know this man, this person she'd just lectured like some prissy know-it-all, but maybe saving his life did give her some rights because it had needed saying—but now it was horrible because she felt the tears welling as she tried to calm down.

Ben sighed. 'I'm sorry, Misty. I was being irresponsibly flippant. Everything you say is right. It was a glib and silly comment and I do regret upsetting you.'

It was his turn to rise on one elbow and look

down into her face. She hoped he couldn't see the tears at the corners of her eyes because suddenly she felt weepy and miserable, no doubt from the huge emotions of the day, but it was embarrassing nonetheless.

Ben noticed. He turned her towards him and gathered her close to encircle her body with his arms. 'I'm sorry, mermaid.'

He pulled her even closer until their cold noses were touching. She could feel his heat between them from her breasts to her hips and again at the knees and his eyes stared into hers, intense and questioning.

'Where have you come from?' Their noses rubbed. 'Why couldn't I have met you when I was young and idealistic, like you?' He frowned as if it was all beyond his understanding. 'How can there be such emotion and connection between two strangers?'

She knew just what he meant. 'I don't know,' she whispered as she watched him shake his head and then wince at the discomfort.

His deep tones caressed her. 'I don't understand, Misty, but I'm very, very grateful. Thank you for saving my life, and putting your precious life at risk to do that. I will always value your gift. Now, hush. It's OK.'

He kissed away the dampness from her cheeks, feather-touched the end of her nose with his mouth, and finally settled his firm lips on hers. And then it all merged.

It was there, that destined connection she'd only

dreamt of in her bed late at night, and there was no doubting it was a gift he hadn't expected either.

He pulled back to stare, perplexed and startled, into her face and then his breath merged seamlessly with hers again as he kissed her until his very soul touched a place she'd known she had but had never dared to open.

He drew her even closer until through the mutual rise and fall of their chests she could feel his heart pound in time to hers. His eyes never left hers as he drew away.

'Rest. We'll both rest,' he said, then he lay back and stared at the ceiling. 'It's been a big day.'

What was he doing? Back off, Ben admonished himself as he rested his head back on the pillow. She'd saved his life and here he was trying to ruin hers. How low could he go?

But what the hell had just happened?

CHAPTER THREE

SURPRISINGLY they both slept. When Ben woke up it was dark outside and Misty lay spooned against him like a kitten. He felt enormously better compared to when he'd gone to sleep, and disturbingly aroused.

When he sat up and glanced back at Misty's sleeping face he felt a spasm in his heart that had nothing to do with almost losing his life. They must have turned at some time in their sleep like an old married couple—but an old married couple who'd never consummated their marriage. He grinned in the darkness. Well, that was a first.

He slid from the bed before his body got more bright ideas and he slipped into the en suite before she woke up and enticed him beyond reason. She wouldn't have to do much.

He planted his hands on the sink and stared into the mirror. His eyes stared back sardonically. Down, boy.

When he ran his hand over the bump on his head he could tell the swelling had almost gone. His chest looked angry in interesting strips but dry from the antibiotic powder Misty had put on.

When he peered into his eyes his pupils seemed equal and he wasted a couple of seconds trying to see the dilation response before he frowned at the hopelessness of trying to catch a pupil reaction on his own face. Idiot. Of course he couldn't. But anything to stop his mind wandering back into the bedroom next door.

'Are you OK, Ben?' Misty's voice came through the door and he looked into the mirror to warn himself to behave.

'Fine, thanks. Be out in a sec,' he said. 'Right after the cold shower,' he finished under his breath.

When he opened the bathroom door five minutes later she'd straightened the bed and disappeared.

He found her on the veranda, gazing out over the beach. The moon hadn't risen yet but the sky was lightening on the horizon where it would emerge.

'It's beautiful when the moon rises out of the sea,' he said as he stopped beside her and slipped his arm around her shoulders. Her neck was taut under his hand and as he rubbed that tender curve he noticed the nervousness she seemed suddenly afflicted with.

She was having second thoughts on her decision to stay. Well, that was fair enough. Very wise of her.

Reluctantly, his arm slid from her shoulders and he stepped back. So how could he still feel her warmth against his body as if he still held her? Because he wanted her back against him, that's how.

She cupped her hands over her upper arms as if to warm herself, and he forced himself not to pull her back into his arms. No doubt she had some boyfriend to rush off to, or she could even be married with a dozen children.

He smiled to himself at that. Her body hadn't seen a dozen children and she wore no ring. He'd checked those things while holding her as they'd drifted off to sleep. Now, why had he done that?

He needed space between them or he'd initiate something they'd both regret. 'Would you like a drink?'

She seemed ridiculously glad he'd asked, making him realise the strain was on both sides, and he felt her follow him back into the house. 'Do you have juice?' she said.

Even though she walked behind him he could pinpoint her position by how sensitive his skin was. It had never been like that before. Ever.

This fey, amazing young woman, who had captured his imagination when he'd least expected it, might prove rather difficult to forget.

'Your "shack" is impressive,' she said in that warm and wonderful voice of hers, but there was a fragile brightness to hide her awareness of the loss of their closeness and he sighed with regret.

Enough. Stop being self-indulgent, he mocked himself, and forced his voice to lightness. He'd give her a drink and send her on her way. 'If you want to see something really impressive, come and see my refrigerator. It's magnificent. What type of juice would you like?'

She peered at the selection like a kid in an ice-cream parlour, and he enjoyed watching her while she hesitated.

He couldn't help the smile in his voice. 'You could have two different juices if you really wanted.'

Unconsciously his hand lifted to feel the warmth in her cheeks and she darted a startled look at him, embarrassed. So her pale skin still blushed easily. A natural redhead. God, her cheek was like silk under his fingers, just like the rest of her.

'Mango juice, thanks,' she said quickly. She took the bottle and turned away from him so that his hand fell.

Ben sighed and closed the wall-sized chrome door, and leaned his forehead against the cold steel for a moment. What was he doing?

Don't touch her again, you idiot, he thought as he closed his eyes because he couldn't bear to hurt someone again and his life was as complicated as ever.

He had to tell her to go. That he'd be fine. That it would be better for her if she left. He opened his eyes and turned to face her.

She wasn't there. The room was empty and the juice stood unopened on the sea chest.

He walked through to the veranda. She wasn't there either, and he glanced down the stairs. The un-mistakable sound of her vehicle door as it closed echoed the emptiness he hadn't realised she'd leave behind. He'd always had that emptiness but it hadn't mattered before. Could he be alone again?

Suddenly he didn't think he could.

The diesel engine came to life and he had no control over his feet as they turned to the stairs. The next thing he knew he was beside her Jeep window.

'Be with me,' he said, and he saw the moment she began to think about accepting and he swore to himself he wouldn't let her down. Please, don't let me hurt her, he prayed, and he couldn't believe that he'd dared to dream again.

His fingers reached through the window of their own accord and turned the key. The engine died.

Silence surrounded them, except for the waves on the shore and the gulls overhead…and the pounding in his heart.

She looked at him with those glorious witch's eyes of hers and he could feel himself drowning, which was ironic considering what the day had held.

He held out his hand. 'Come with me. Please.'

She saw there in his eyes the quiet hope that made her wish to be as daring as he was, as positive as he was, that this wouldn't end in futile regrets.

Misty raised her hand towards his and then stopped.

What was she doing? She knew what would happen if she went back into the house with him. She wanted it to happen but she needed to think sensibly about this. Safely and non-emotionally after one of the most emotional days she'd ever had. And realized she was terrified. This interlude would end. She longed to burn boats, jump off the cliff to uncertainty and yet they had barely talked. Just felt…and kissed.

It was an impossible dream. They both had lives, and commitments, and uncertainties, and they'd met this once by the merest chance. She needed to leave before he imprinted himself further on her soul.

She lifted her fingers to the ignition and the metal felt cold and hard as she turned the key. 'I don't think so. Take care, Ben.' She glanced once more at his face and the expression suddenly stripped from his features as if someone had turned off a light.

Right decision, she thought, and forced herself to drive away.

Right decision, Ben thought. Sensible girl.

She was gone and Ben lay alone in his big bed with just the scent of her skin on the pillow beside him and emptiness in his heart as he said goodbye. Sensible, sensible girl.

The sound of a ringtone filled the room.

His phone.

His breath shuddered in his throat as he sat up, and he shook his head at the person on the other end. 'I'll come,' he said into his phone.

He looked out the window at the rolling ocean and his chin lifted. Impossible dream, he thought, uncannily echoing Misty as he shut his phone and reached for his shirt.

CHAPTER FOUR

MISTY didn't remember much about the drive to Lyrebird Lake. The memory of Ben in her rear-view mirror watching her go just seemed to get bigger the further away from Ben that she drove. Had she missed the opportunity to experience life and love with someone who could have been the one man for her?

She'd never be sure and he didn't even know her last name.

She stayed the night at a motel, she couldn't even remember which town, and it had been hard to get up that morning and drive further west. But now, as she drove through the wide and tree-lined streets of Lyrebird Lake, her spirits lifted.

It was time for her to start her new life. Just like Ben needed to. She hoped he would find happiness.

The car turned into the driveway of her brother's house and she sighed and reached over to turn off the engine. She'd done the right thing. She had.

'Welcome to Lyrebird Lake.' Misty heard the

words and accepted the hug Montana offered. She ignored the feeling that her heart would probably never speak to her again.

It was wonderful to see her best friend again but there was no doubt the excitement of her new home had dimmed and she hoped Montana didn't notice the effort it took to smile.

'I bet you didn't see this in our future.' Andy laughed as he also hugged her.

Her big brother's arms were just what she needed to make her feel strong again. 'There were a lot of things I didn't see,' she said, and tried to smile.

Andy put her away from him and frowned at her searchingly. 'What's happened to you?'

'Shh, love,' Montana said, and Misty watched with wry amusement as her friend rested her hand on Andy's arm. 'Let your sister get her breath. We have plenty of time.'

'Assuming the phone doesn't ring and I don't get called out,' Andy muttered, as he carried Misty's bags into their house and she followed with her arm hooked in Montana's.

They shared a glance and smiled. Men, the look said, but they both loved his care. 'He's still looking for a locum to share the workload because he won't let me out of his sight until I have this baby,' Montana whispered.

Montana, a widow at the time of her first baby's birth two years ago, had been alone at a mountain retreat when labour had begun rapidly without warning. Unable to drive any further, Montana had pulled over before she could reach the hospital, and at sunrise had delivered her daughter alone on an escarpment.

One of Misty's premonitions had urged her brother to search for and find Montana and her new baby. Andy had found more than the two people he'd been looking for. He had found his love. This time Montana's birth experience would be different because Andy would be there for her.

Misty was there too, now, and she would keep Montana safe as well.

Half an hour later Misty could feel the healing from the sense of family and love around her and she began to relax. She'd done the right thing to choose Lyrebird Lake over a man who had only briefly touched her life. No matter that the touch had been so iridescent.

The three of them were seated on the veranda of Montana and Andy's newly built home and the outdoor sail overhead shaded them from the fierce Queensland sun. The breeze from the lake stirred the air with tantalising wisps of coolness.

Queensland weather was different from that of New South Wales but she would get used to the heat. It was very different from the ocean and Ben.

Misty glanced inwards to the open-plan house— a sprawling building of light and polished floors and large windows all shaded by verandas. It made her think of another house with polished floorboards and a different kind of heat. 'Your house is beautiful and yet it's very much a home.'

Andy raised his eyebrows indulgently. 'Wait until Dawn wakes up. Our daughter can demolish it in minutes.'

'Imagine the chaos when her new brother or sister arrives.' Misty glanced at Montana's rounded stomach. 'You'll have twice as much mess to clean up.'

She watched her two favourite people in the world exchange loving glances and she stifled a sigh. If only it were that easy.

'So tell me who broke your heart and I'll go and wring his neck.' The concerned look on Andy's face brought a hiccough of laughter and a sting of tears to her eyes.

So it showed. Andy had always looked after her, always cared and worried that his little sister was OK, especially after their mother had died.

Misty had been able to read his mind for years and he worried she avoided relationships in case her gift spoilt them. She'd wondered if being married would change that care, but obviously not.

She swallowed away the prickle of tears in her throat. 'What makes you think my heart is broken? And why does it have to be a man?'

Andy blinked and she laughed with only a trace of bitterness at his confusion.

'Yes, it's a man,' she said before he bogged down in some improbable scenario.

'Well, you waited all this time to find someone. Why couldn't you have waited a little bit longer? Found someone at the lake and settled here for good?'

Fat chance, the way she felt at the moment, Misty thought. 'I'm afraid it's too late for that now.'

'Is there a possibility for it all to work out?' Montana's quiet voice questioned, and Misty looked at her friend before she shook her head.

'All what?'

Misty compared the understated wealth of the beach house to her modest financial security, Ben's world-weary experience compared to her girlish optimism, her passion for birth and Ben's revulsion for obstetrics, and finally the fact that she hadn't even told him her surname. She had no doubt they would remain ships in the night.

'No chance.' She shook her head and accepted the finality with a new stab of loss. 'If he'd been less a man of the world—if we'd had a little more in common—he would have been perfect. It was also far too intense for stability, just a fantasy, and I was kidding myself.'

She felt again the touch of Ben's hand on hers. 'It was so strange, though. The moment when we met, I felt a shift, as if I'd suddenly realised I'd only ever been half of myself. It's all a bit raw and of course I will survive.' She lifted her chin. 'But with him I felt

I could achieve anything.' She sighed. 'In a strange way he made me feel like a queen.'

'Of course you can still achieve anything! And you've always been a queen to me,' Andy said gruffly.

Montana reached across and squeezed Misty's hand. 'That's why I love your brother.'

She smiled at her husband and then back at Misty. 'With this man, though, the attraction between you both must have been potent to affect you as it did.'

Misty met her eyes. 'I left Sydney normal and arrived up here totally different. He's changed me in just a few hours and I'll probably never see him again. The impact he's had on me is ridiculous.'

Andy rubbed the back of his neck as he searched for the right words. 'Let me get this straight. On the way here you had a one-night stand with some bloke you've never met before.' Andy shook his head. 'And he didn't make arrangements to see you again?'

Misty sighed. 'It wasn't quite that simple and I didn't have a one-night stand.'

'At least that's good news,' Andy growled.

'Andy, love.' Montana frowned her husband down. 'Let Misty talk.'

Misty blew a kiss to her brother for his championing but all the wishing in the world didn't change the facts. 'We met under exceptional circumstances. We never had the chance to find out where it could go.'

'Why not?' Montana asked quietly. It was unlike Montana to persist. It was as if she understood that

Misty needed to come to grips with what had happened, and Misty appreciated that. In some masochistic way it helped to confirm it had been nothing more than a dream.

'There was no future in it. We don't know anything about each other. Our stars collided for a day and that was all.'

'It must have been some collision,' Andy said.

She looked at Montana. 'He was knocked off the rocks into the sea, and when I arrived he'd almost drowned.' She shuddered. 'I pulled him to shore and he wasn't breathing.'

Andy sat up straight, appalled Misty had been in danger. 'You risked your life for this guy?'

'Always so fearless, Misty. But that must have been horrible.' Montana understood and her calm voice soothed her husband into silence.

She too easily recalled Ben's lifeless body on the beach and glanced at Andy. 'I had my surfboard. But even now I can still see him.' Misty shivered at the memory.

Andy looked as though he fancied the idea of Ben's lifeless body and she swallowed a giggle. As a big brother he was sweet, but he didn't understand. If only life were that simple.

'All I know about him is that he wrote a textbook.' She avoided Ben's profession in case Andy knew him.

Andy nodded his head. 'Of course', he said sarcastically. 'He's self-indulgent and can't swim.

Sounds like a hero to me. And he preys on good Samaritans.'

Misty laughed at her brother's simplistic image. 'He'd have swum if he hadn't been knocked out on the rocks after he saved a bird.'

Andy crossed his arms. 'Then he's clumsy.'

The two friends looked at each other and both ignored Andy's final outburst. 'He's met you now,' Montana said. 'He'll find you again.'

'Thank you, Montana,' Misty said as she looked at a scowling Andy. 'It's not going to happen, but thank you.'

Ben climbed the rocks under the lighthouse but all he could think of was a month ago and the sweet taste of Misty. A huge change from thinking about the mess his life was.

She was lucky she hadn't stayed. He ran his hand over the uneven surface of the cliff as if he'd find the answer there.

He just wanted to go find her at that lake she'd spoken about so passionately. The fact that he didn't know where she was at that moment was of no concern. He had enough clues and he'd find her if he decided to.

But would it be fair to her? He picked up a loose stone and spun it out over the waves towards the sunrise. Of course it wasn't.

Even walking in his favourite place in the world,

as he tried to move on and forget her, every emerald-green rock pool still reminded him of her. Every swirl of seaweed splayed and dipped like Misty's passion-red hair in the water.

Maybe he'd imagined the connection between them? Or maybe the peace he'd glimpsed with her could help him? The sweetness of her scent and the feel of her softness against him was certainly an inducement.

How could two people who barely knew each other be spiralled into the almost mystical connection of that afternoon and not end up together again?

Because she didn't need his baggage and he didn't believe in fairy-tales. He was a grown man, not a callow youth. Ben watched the water slap against the barnacles on the breakwall and considered knocking his stupid head against them.

Forget her. She'd stunned him with the generosity of her open heart and he'd been fighting against his instincts ever since.

But a month ago his life had almost ended and he'd spent the last four weeks sorting the flotsam of disasters that had been drowning him even more than the sea had on the day Misty had appeared.

Yes, his daughter still needed him now, more than ever. Would Misty understand that? Even when Tammy wasn't really his daughter? But watching from a distance hadn't kept Tammy safe.

It was time he was the real father he wanted to be

and take a stand. He'd wanted Tammy to come and live with him in the past, at least until she finished school and he could keep her safe. He'd even offered to move somewhere, anywhere, so she could start again fresh and innocent of the worry her mother had heaped on her young shoulders before she'd died.

But Tammy had elected to stay at boarding school and now she was pregnant and had told no one until she had been almost eight months. Lord knows how she had managed that but the school knew now and Tammy had to leave in her second-last year, just like her mother had.

But Tammy was his priority now and with school no longer an option she'd have to come to him, because her vague and flighty grandmother had proved unreliable. And he'd make sure she saw that. She needed to get away from the crowd she'd managed to become a part of without his or the school's knowledge.

With that crowd was no way for a young girl to live her life especially in her condition, not knowing which was the father of his grandchild he couldn't strangle them all, and it was time to put his foot down. He and his 'daughter' would move somewhere safe. Away. So why not to Lyrebird Lake?

Misty didn't deserve the confused and bitter daughter of Bridget's but maybe she could help. Maybe she could help both of them. And he had Misty's word that it was the best place for any woman to have her baby.

CHAPTER FIVE

FROM the first the tiny Lyrebird Lake Hospital and its midwifery unit welcomed Misty with open arms.

That warm inclusion helped salve Misty's pain after the extraordinary effect Ben had had on her and the emptiness she hadn't expected to be left with.

To avoid a gap in service when Montana went on maternity leave, Misty took over as much as she could so Montana could finish up without feeling she'd deserted her clients.

Unlike a maternity unit in a larger hospital, Lyrebird Lake ran on a caseload of antenatal women with uncomplicated pregnancies. Each midwife established a close rapport with her own clients and both sides were reluctant to change.

The town had accepted this new service with heartfelt relief from the previous only option of a hospital stay eighty kilometres away from their families and the fragmented shared care they'd received there.

For the midwives there was a rewarding completion in the circle of care not offered by the larger hospitals.

Of course, any complicated pregnancies or births were assessed by Andy or a locum doctor and transferred to the larger hospital at the base by ambulance for obstetric intervention.

Even then, once stable, the woman and her baby could return to the lake prior to discharge home if she wanted to, and connect up with her midwife again.

But yesterday's news had hung over her all night. The needs of the town had grown considerably with the local coal mine now in full operation, and the workload continued to increase. Ben was coming to the lake—today. The mine's new housing estate had opened on the shores of the lake, ensuring the midwifery unit functioned more days than it was closed.

Babies arrived calmly and naturally and then, tucked in their mother's or father's arms, sailed serenely out the door to go home.

Montana, who'd set up the unit with Andy's blessing and support, became one of Misty's own caseload clients on her last day.

Sara, one of the other two midwives, handed over her care to Misty, although she would remain the back-up carer.

'So Montana is due in four weeks.' Sara grinned at her former client. 'She's very easy to get along with. It's her second baby and she has great resource skills for birth.' Sara ceremoniously handed over the file.

Misty laughed. 'I did hear she can be a little re-luctant to come in when she starts labour, though.' Misty glanced at Montana, who rolled her eyes.

'Very funny, you two,' Montana said. 'I assure you I'm coming in. Andy has the car at the ready and never lets me out of his sight.'

In fact, Andy had come to take Montana home on her last day and he gathered her close to him with a soft smile.

'Ready to finally take it easy,' he said as he took Montana's bag from her to carry.

'So you have your wife home for a while,' Misty teased her brother and he grinned back.

'Such a hardship.'

'You'll really hate being called out now.'

'I've got a locum,' Andy said smugly, and Montana and Misty both looked at him in surprise.

That had been sudden, Misty thought, and her hand fell to her stomach, which suddenly clutched with nerves.

'This guy is actually an obstetrician—rang out of the blue and offered to start today. The paperwork's through and clear.' Andy was smug.

'That seems a bit eager,' Montana commented, but she couldn't hide her delight that her husband would have a lessened workload.

'Does this eager beaver have a name?' Misty tried to keep her voice nonchalant but the wobble was there for her to hear at least.

'Ben Moore. A widower. He's been out of obstetrics for a couple of years but we don't do obstetrics here anyway, do we, girls?' Andy teased them back.

It was good to see her brother so happy, Misty told herself as a flutter of skittish seagulls, reminiscent of another day, seemed to have landed in her stomach.

Of course Andy had jumped at the chance to be able to spend more time with Montana at the end of her pregnancy. It was crazy to feel trapped and nervous when the news was so good for her brother but...

Ben was coming to the lake. It had been a month and of course she was over that silly thing she had for him.

Luckily, as it was her first morning in charge she could keep busy on the phone with the pregnant women on her caseload, and she didn't have time to dwell on what it might mean that Ben would be here soon. All the time, though, at the back of her mind sat Andy's news.

Andy had said Ben would arrive some time today. What time? What would she say? What would he say? At the very least he couldn't say she'd been chasing him.

Why now when she had just started to think of him less? Could it possibly be a coincidence he'd decided to come here now, just when Andy needed him, or had he followed her?

She sniffed. It was no coincidence and she had no

idea what he had in mind. She needed less speculation and more concentration on the job. But despite all the sensible reminders she couldn't completely dampen the flicker of hope that he'd missed her and had followed her with a view to getting to know her better.

An hour later when the door to the ward opened down the hall her hand stilled as she bent to tuck the end of the clean sheet under the mattress. Was it him? Already? She wasn't prepared enough, and she looked around frantically as if she could hide.

Stop it! Misty breathed out and waited—calmly, she assured herself—for whoever it was to enter, close the door, and find her.

She forced herself to resume her task but in that frozen moment of intrusion it was strange how suddenly all her senses seemed to have come alive. Time slowed to aching fragments of seconds and the creases in her hands seemed suddenly enlarged and ugly when she stared down at her fingers.

She could clearly identify the tang of bleach on the crisp, white hospital sheet and feel the slight stiffness in the cotton as it slid coldly beneath her fingers.

In slow motion she squared the corner of the sheet and tucked it under the mattress before she straightened and strained her ears for more sound.

The expected hail from her visitor didn't come. Only the world outside the windows drifted in—the passing cars, the call of birds, a scratchy rustle of a branch against the wall outside the room.

No footsteps? She frowned. Where was he? 'Hello.' Her voice sounded much more uncertain than she'd expected.

'Who's there?' she called, and for a split second Ben's arrival seemed less certain and a nasty alternative occurred to her. She began to edge back against the wall and unconsciously her hand slid protectively across her heart.

Finally the door swung closed again and then she heard the footsteps she'd waited for. Purposeful, not threatening or sinister, somebody who was looking for a midwife, and her shoulders dropped with relief.

'Hello yourself.' The cadence echoed her own memory of the sound of Ben's voice and she let the sound wash over her with unexpected relief.

'I thought no one was here,' he said.

Ben wasn't the sinister intruder she'd conjured up in her imagination and she took a step towards him before she remembered a month had passed since she'd spoken to him last. And she didn't know why he was there.

Ben must have seen the tension on her face because his eyes narrowed as he glanced around. 'Misty? Are you OK?'

She sighed, heavily, still faint with tension. 'It's you.'

He tilted his head and his gaze roamed over her face, as if reimprinting her on his memory. 'Who else did you think it might be?'

'No idea. Just had a silly fright. My nerves are shot,' she said, and laughed shakily before she dragged her eyes away from the intensity of his.

Ben looked so large and vital and handsome and so, so out of her reach. How could she tell this stranger she'd been thinking of him day and night for a month?

'I didn't think you had nerves,' he teased. He stepped closer. 'Your face is pale,' he said, and just that sympathy made her want to lay her head on his chest, and when he reached across to stroke her cheek, the single touch evoked the morning at the beach house in full sensory force.

She flinched at the heat that transmitted itself through her skin and spread a surge of warmth across her face and neck like a flash fire. Her brain urged her back against the wall and thankfully the plaster was cold enough against her spine to combat the conflagration that was spreading under the surface of her skin.

With her obvious recoil Ben's hand drew back and froze in mid-air before he tucked it in his pocket out of sight as if ashamed of the contact.

'I'm sorry.' He widened the gap between their bodies with a further step back and then glanced around as if seeing the room for the first time.

The silence stretched between them and Misty couldn't remember a time when she'd felt more uncomfortable.

Finally Ben spoke. 'So, no patients in here?' His comment hung, superfluous, in the empty ward but at least he'd tried to fill the gap in conversation and she gestured to the half-made bed.

'I've just discharged the last, as you can see.' Great help with the dialogue, she mocked herself, but that was all she could manage right then. She was too busy trying to control the thudding in her chest.

It had been a little over a month since she'd seen him but in that time she'd grown so accustomed to recalling his bare chest in her mind's eye that she was startled by his tailored clothes.

The white of his shirt shone brightly against the tan of his neck, and his forearms looked strong and brown under the rolled-up sleeves. The fitted design of his buttoned shirt complemented the breadth of his chest far too effectively and she looked away and then down at his feet.

Definitely not bare, they were encased in expensive Italian shoes and topped by tailored grey trousers that made her think of city specialists, not locum country doctors.

She wondered suddenly how he'd find working in an environment so different from that of a city hospital.

The silence lengthened and then his voice drifted softly across from where he stood. 'I'm sorry, Misty.'

She tilted her chin and met his gaze. Finally she had control. 'For what, Ben?' Her tone was cool. 'I'm the one who left.'

'For pressuring you when I shouldn't have.' He glanced around the empty room again. 'Can we talk about that?'

She knew he could see the barriers she'd erected so it was a silly question, but still his asking shocked her. 'Not here or now, no!'

Ben half laughed in frustration. 'When?' The woman would drive him mad with the way she looked at him as if she'd never felt any connection between them. But he could feel it shivering between them like a wall of nerve endings, waving in the breeze like the branches of a willow tree.

Ignore it. Pretend it wasn't there. She could and so could he. He had to ignore it to because he'd really come here for his daughter. Not for Misty. He'd keep telling himself that and eventually it would be true.

'When should we talk about it? Probably never, but I'll let you know,' she said, and looked away.

That intrigued him. What didn't she want him to see in her face?

She resumed the conversation as if whatever had bothered her had been mastered. Her eyes met his and now he couldn't look away.

'At the moment I'm wondering why you're here.' She tilted her delightful chin at him. 'Why are you here, Ben?'

'You're bristling,' he said conversationally. She wasn't as calm as she made out and that made him feel a little better. 'I think we should talk about that later as well.'

The sound of a vehicle and the rattle of gravel outside heralded a new client and Misty looked away with what he considered disproportionate relief. 'In that case, I've work to do,' she said.

'Work?' She wanted him gone. Well, he wasn't quite ready. 'Sounds interesting. After what you told me at the beach house. Could I see how it pans out? Then I'll slip away.'

She didn't answer. 'I'll check out the admission CTG. See what the trace's like,' Ben murmured, and he drifted to the nurses' station and picked up a file as if to check for something.

Misty looked at him strangely then shook her head. There was no doubt he'd exasperated her again. Now what had he said?

'We don't have a foetal monitor here, Ben.'

No CTG? 'What do you mean?'

'It's a low-risk unit, remember,' she said. 'We only have low-risk women and hooking them up to a machine to electronically listen to a baby we can hear very well other ways is crazy. Our clinical skills give us all the information we need to know.'

His hospital had always used them. They had been part of the protocol of every birth. He'd assumed Lyrebird Lake would have a machine somewhere, in a cupboard at least. He'd never even heard of a place delivering babies without one. The CTG machine allowed a baby's heart rate to be traced at the same time as the mother's contractions to indicate the baby's response to the stresses of labour.

He breathed deeply. It would be OK. He supposed the trace didn't guarantee anything, and even when you could hold the results in your hand it didn't mean all was going to go well.

He caught himself at that thought. These women and babies were healthy, she'd said. He was doing it again. Thinking negative thoughts.

'Not even an admission trace.' He hoped she didn't hear the unhappy note in his voice that even he could hear. This place had to be good for his obstetric soul.

'Don't have one, don't want one. We'll talk about this another time.'

He couldn't imagine obstetrics without electronic screening tools for risk. 'What if you hear the baby's heart rate slow down after a contraction while you're listening?'

'CHICKEN,' she said. Ben blinked. Surely she hadn't just called him a chicken?

He felt as if he'd been slapped. He'd discovered Misty's feet of clay and his stomach plummeted. Unsafe practitioner? Surely not? He couldn't work here. Not in this environment. He stepped further away from her but she went on.

'It's an emergency mnemonic, Ben. "C.H." stands for Change Her position. "I" stands for put an IV cannula in and Infuse or Increase her fluid load.

"KE" stands for KEep listening after every contraction. "N" stands for Notify…' Her voice trailed off.

Ben's head was spinning. C.H.I.C.K.E.N? He blinked.

Misty sighed. She'd seen his horror when she'd given him the mnemonic. For her it had been a reflex answer from their emergency practices.

He'd actually thought she'd dared him to play roulette with other people's lives.

If she'd had more time she'd have been hurt but later she would mull over it. Why had he been so quick to damn her practice ethic? Did he honestly think looking after women at one of the most important times in their lives was a thrill ride?

She shook her head to rid herself of the thoughts. Later. She'd sort him out.

Misty frowned at him but then she heard the door open. 'I usually ring the nurse, but you can stay if you want, seeing as your paperwork came through.' She shrugged and tried to ignore him as she went forward to greet the woman and her anxious partner.

'You're Montana's friend?' the man said, and when Misty nodded, he sighed with relief.

'Cherry's waters have broken and she's been wanting to push for the last five minutes in the car. I was that scared she'd pop it out on my seat covers.'

That would be Cherry Glover, Misty thought to herself as she mentally reviewed those 'at term' ladies the unit expected.

'Looks like you made it just in time, then. You must be Ritchie.'

She turned to the woman. 'Hello, Cherry. We'll have you all set in no time. Come through this way.'

She paused at the desk and scooped up Cherry's file. 'This is Dr Moore. He's our new locum and will be staying as the second person because I don't have a nurse at the moment.'

Ben waved and smiled, acknowledging his recruitment, even as Misty moved on to focus on the job at hand.

She'd only read Cherry's notes that morning and her case was as uncomplicated as all the women booked to the unit were. No risk factors, healthy-sized baby, no blood-pressure problems prior to labour and this was her third healthy pregnancy.

Ritchie was probably right. It was quite on the cards that Cherry was ready to 'pop' this one out. She smiled to herself as Cherry's next contraction was accompanied by a few grunty breaths on Cherry's part. No need to check if she was ready.

Ben fiddled with the baby trolley while Misty helped Cherry climb awkwardly out of her damp clothes and wrapped her in a sarong.

When her next contraction had eased Misty asked if she was up to climbing onto the bed for a quick abdominal examination and so Misty could listen to the baby's heartbeat.

'Just to check baby's lie. We can use the Doppler with you standing after that.'

'No problem, as long as you're quick,' Cherry said, and Misty saw Ben stiffen out of the corner of her eye. Now, what was up with him?

When Cherry lay down Misty quickly palpated the woman's shiny round abdomen and easily identified the foetal back and the descent of the foetal head into the pelvis.

Everything was great. 'OK, your baby's head is down and engaged nicely. He or she is facing the right way and I'll just have a quick listen.'

Misty counted for a minute with the Pinard's, and as she turned her ear to Cherry's abdomen she found herself facing Ben. The expression on his face, though quickly hidden, had shown disbelief and even a tinge of sardonic amusement at her archaic instrument.

'We use this first,' she said to Cherry, but really to Mr Modern Age in the corner, 'to confirm baby's position by the baby's heart rate. It sounds different using this to the mother's pulse. Sometimes the electronic equipment can hear the baby all over the place.' Sound principles, Ben, so get used to it! She hoped her eyes conveyed the message.

He inclined his head so at least he was receptive to her rebuke, she thought grimly, and she straightened and concentrated on her client.

Once she'd confirmed the baby's lie to her satisfaction she placed the hand-held Doppler on Cherry's stomach low down near her pubic bone so the parents could hear the clop, clop, clop of the baby's heart-beat as it filled the room.

Ritchie smiled with relief and Misty grinned, too. 'Your little passenger is very happy in there, even though you've pulled the plug on them.'

She helped Cherry stand up again and smiled at Cherry's sigh from the awkwardness of lying down during the serious end of labour.

Even Ben should be able to see how much easier it was for Cherry in an upright position. 'Do you want to lean on the bed?'

At Cherry's nod Misty raised the level of the bed so that Cherry could stand and lean against it without bending too much.

Misty guided Ritchie behind his wife to massage her lower back in firm circular motions while Cherry breathed through the pains.

When he was at his task, Misty turned to her own responsibilities. She connected the overhead heater and completed her own check of the baby's emergency trolley then readied her basic equipment for the birth.

She was still aware of Ben as he leaned against the rear wall of the room, quietly watching.

Concentrate, she chided herself as she began to mentally list her tasks. All she needed was two clamps for the cord and scissors for Ritchie to cut between the clamps, a dish to catch the placenta and a warm towel and blanket for baby.

No drugs to hasten the placenta, she remembered. 'You've declined the injection after the birth, Cherry. Is that right?'

Cherry sighed as the next pain started. 'I don't want it unless I have to.'

'Have you explained the rationale for oxytocin, Sister?' Ben asked quietly.

Misty froze and then glanced quickly at Cherry and Ritchie, but they didn't seem to have heard as the woman's breathing increased in tempo.

'We discuss it at antenatal visits, yes,' Misty said, and then added, 'A woman's choice.' Then she ignored him and ran warm water into a bowl before she slipped her gloves on to dip a washcloth into the warm fluid and wait.

Cherry moaned and Ritchie yelped as a small trickle of blood ran down his wife's leg. 'She's haemorrhaging,' he gasped, and Misty smiled.

'That's the show. It's OK, Ritchie. That "shows" Cherry's cervix, or the opening at the bottom of the uterus, is opening and her time is near. After she's had the baby I'll get you to put the electric bed down to low level again so Cherry can lie back.'

'You mean she's having it standing up?' Ritchie cast a horrified look in Misty's direction before his wife recalled his attention.

'Fabulous,' Ben whispered with the tiniest hint of sarcasm, and Misty frowned. One more negative comment and she'd ask him to leave.

'Keep rubbing!' Cherry's command was almost a growl and Misty bit her lip to stop her smile again. Cherry was running this show, not Ben Moore.

'If Cherry didn't want to be in this position,' she said to Ritchie, and—without looking at him—to Ben, 'she'd move. Everything is fine. Now, do you see the controls for the bed, there, Ritchie?' Misty pointed. 'I'll tell you when to move it back down.'

Ritchie gulped at that much responsibility and Cherry moaned loudly.

Misty slipped in next to Ritchie. She placed her warm towel for the baby on the bed beside her client.

'OK, Cherry,' she said. 'Nice and easy. I'm just going to put my hand down here with a warm wash-cloth to help that burning feeling as baby's head comes through.'

She felt the baby's occiput bulge under her hand as Cherry pushed, and suddenly the head was out.

'Whoops. That was quick.' Misty smiled. 'That's great, Cherry, your baby's head's born. Take some little breaths if the pain has gone or push again if you need to.'

'Oh, my God,' Ritchie muttered distantly as his knees wobbled and he swayed limply against Misty as his legs gave way.

'Just sit for a minute, mate.' Ben's calm voice came from behind Misty's shoulder as he nudged Ritchie into the chair beside the bed and the new father collapsed. Ben firmly placed Ritchie's head between his knees and bounced him twice.

'Take a few breaths, mate.'

At least Ben could do something constructive. Misty grinned without turning as she kept one hand on the baby's head. She flicked open the warm towel with the other and dried the little scalp as she waited.

Cherry pushed again and baby rotated until a shoulder appeared, then the rest of baby unfolded into Misty's towel-wrapped hands in a flurry of limbs.

Misty slipped the baby still joined by the umbilical cord through Cherry's legs to Ben, who had appeared usefully beside Cherry at the front. He gently wiped the little body before passing her naked baby up to Cherry.

Cherry dropped her sarong unselfconsciously to bare her skin for baby, who mewled like a little kitten and then settled when she was snuggled against her mother's warm skin.

'What is it?' Ritchie's voice was muffled from his position but cracked with emotion and Misty and Ben waited quietly for Cherry to look.

'It's my girl,' Cherry sobbed as she hugged the squirming baby to her chest. 'Hello, Phoebe.'

'Just push that button and lower the bed so Cherry can sit down, Ritchie.' She glanced at the man beside her but he'd returned his head between his knees.

'I've got it,' Ben murmured from behind her left ear, and the whirr of the bed mechanism underlined his presence. She was glad he was there because with his scepticism he needed to see everything was normal. He'd even been a little handy.

Cherry eased onto the bed with her baby against her chest and Ben draped a blanket over both of them.

After a few minutes Misty lifted the edge of the blanket and offered Ritchie the scissors. 'Are you going to cut the cord, Ritchie?'

'Can't.' Ritchie's voice was muffled from his hands over his face. 'Maybe in a minute.'

'No rush.' Misty tucked the blanket back as they waited. After a further few minutes Ritchie reached across and Misty showed him where to cut.

'I need to push again.' Cherry knew what came next as the placenta was delivered into the dish Misty held.

Misty held up the bowl. 'Did you want to see this, Cherry? These are incredible things. I always think of placentas as amazing little heart-lung machines that incubate babies beautifully.'

'I've never looked before,' Cherry said, and she craned her neck curiously when Misty held up the thin membranous bag.

'This is where baby lived inside you,' Misty expanded the membrane so the pale balloon shaped bag hung as if baby was still inside.

'The shiny side is inside the bag and you can see the place where the umbilical cord is connected.'

'Wow. Check this out, Ritchie.' Cherry was impressed but Ritchie kept his head averted now he'd lifted it enough to see his daughter.

'No way.'

Misty smiled at Cherry and took the placenta away.

Ritchie shuddered. 'I'd much rather look at my daughter.' He stroked his baby's cheek. 'Phoebe. She's like you, honey.'

He smiled tearily at Cherry. 'Gorgeous.' And he stood up carefully and leaned over and kissed his wife. 'Women are incredible.' He shook his head in disbelief that it was all over and his daughter was safely in front of him.

Misty tucked the warmed blanket around Cherry's shoulders after ensuring her uterus had started contracting to control bleeding. She quickly checked Cherry's blood pressure and pulse while Ben listened to Phoebe's lungs, thankfully without disturbing her, as she nudged at her mother's breast.

'We'll leave you three to get acquainted,' Misty said quietly. 'I'll just be outside if you need anything.'

The new parents nodded as Misty and Ben left the room and the door shut quietly.

CHAPTER SIX

'AT THE lake we don't appreciate negative people in the birthing centre, Ben.'

Misty was furious and Ben blinked because he hadn't seen it coming. The green sparks from her glare were no doubt burning holes in his forehead as he listened and he didn't see how he could have missed it in the room. 'Was I?' He hadn't realised it.

Misty put the chart down carefully, though he had the impression she wanted to slam it through the desk. Amazing how much more powerful her restraint was. The woman was never boring.

'There were a few sceptical comments I could have done without,' she said quietly. 'I'm hoping Cherry didn't hear them.'

'I apologise.' He thought back. He may have muttered something about the patient standing up. It wasn't something he would choose as an optimum position for the person actually catching the baby. 'Did she choose vertical or did you?'

Misty compressed her lips, which only served to draw attention to something he was trying not to think about—her gorgeous mouth. Consciously he cut the thought off. That was not why he was there and he was sorry if he'd upset her.

Misty closed her eyes briefly as if exasperated with him. 'Did you have your ears shut when she sighed with relief at getting off the bed?'

He thought about that. Maybe. 'And, antenatally, do you encourage no injections after the birth?' He raised his eyebrows sceptically. 'Or do all the women mystically come to the same conclusion and decline off their own bats?'

'They choose, Ben. That's what this place is all about. Choice.' She looked at him. 'You'll have to get used to it or this isn't the place for you.'

She meant that. She really did. He thought about the conversation, about what he'd just witnessed and what he knew about Misty—the woman who had saved his life and asked nothing in return.

And the baby's outcome? 'Well, the birth was incredible. Thank you for allowing me to stay.' He really was glad of the opportunity to get an early impression of how they did things here.

'I guess it's such a different style from my last hospital it will take me a few days to get used to it.'

It was Misty's turn to be nonplussed. Ben appeared bemused, as if he'd forgotten how natural birth could be, which didn't make sense when she knew he must have seen hundreds of babies enter the world.

She frowned at the underlying confusion in his eyes. She'd always imagined he'd be in absolute control of his emotions and she'd been surprised at his intrusive comments during the birth.

Though he'd been helpful at the end. She supposed it was a mental swing from being the primary obstetrician on a big ward to a midwife's helper here, but it was something he needed to change if her unit was going to remain as peaceful as it normally was.

'Cherry was amazing,' she said instead, and tried to lighten the atmosphere. 'Thanks for steering Ritchie into the chair. It's always distracting when a dad faints beside me.'

The more he thought about it the more Ben's mind was grappling with something he seemed to have lost sight of years ago. The joy of birth. 'The least I could do,' he said but his thoughts were elsewhere.

It had been far too long since he'd seen a normal birth, a healthy woman and no interference from the birth attendant. But the element of risk when everything was left to nature would take some getting used to.

A flicker of familiar unease and the darkness he'd like to have left behind caught up with him. They were still playing with life here and he'd seen what bad outcomes could do to people. 'I'm not happy about the lack of injection after the birth.'

Misty looked up at him as if he'd just blasphemed and he found his mouth twitching at what was becoming a standard response from her.

The edge was back in her voice and he realised he'd ignited her zeal more than he'd intended. 'The medication is there if we need it,' she said. 'But we seldom do. Doesn't it make you think of all those women who have interference that don't need it?'

He shook his head. 'No. It makes me think of the controlled randomised studies that prove oxytocin after the birth of the baby decreases the risk of post-partum haemorrhage in hospitals.'

Misty nodded but there was a glint in her eye. 'I think the key word is "hospitals". Why do you think women have more haemorrhages in hospital, Ben?' She raised her finely arched brows. 'Hmmm. I wonder.'

She was daring him to get into a technical discussion with her. No problem, lady, he thought, and mentally rubbed his hands. 'Enlighten me.'

She raised her eyebrows, not one whit intimidated by his confidence that he'd win this one.

'I've already said it. Interference,' she said. 'That's why.'

'Isn't this a hospital?'

'No. It's a birth centre. Women-centred care for healthy pregnant women.'

He thought about her response and conceded that the more qualifications and experience he had, the more the system seemed to thrust him into intervention and diagnostics. Stats might not be as valid here but they were valid where he'd come from. Then again, he hadn't been anywhere like this place in all his time.

This place was amazing but he wasn't going to tell her that. How much specialist antenatal care did they really receive here? 'Did Cherry even have an ultrasound during pregnancy?'

'Andy likes the clients booked here to have one ultrasound at least.' Misty's brows drew together and from the frown he guessed she didn't think the women needed that either. That amused him.

Misty went on. 'They have scans at eighteen weeks into the pregnancy. Other than that we answer ultrasound questions with good antenatal care and hands-on assessment.' There was challenge in the last words. 'As it should be.'

He'd bet their clinical skills were top-notch with all that hands-on experience. 'So how does this place work with staff?'

She grinned at that as if the mention of staff made her smile. Misty was jotting times and names in the birth register and had recovered her good humour. He should take a leaf out of her book and learn to get over things once they were discussed. Maybe he wouldn't have turned into the person he was.

She answered absently. 'I call a second person in for the birth in case they need to go for something or call for help, but otherwise they're only an observer. You have to remember these are low-risk women doing what they are designed to do.' She thought of Montana. 'They could do it on their own if they had to.'

All his misgivings came back. He couldn't banish the spectre of worrying if something went wrong. The spectre of the past. 'So you look after them on your own or with another midwife?'

Misty must have picked up on his unease because a firmer note had entered her voice. 'Or a nurse, or Andy if no one else is around. Now, I guess, you.'

All he could think of were the hordes of people available in the hospital he'd worked at. Midwives, nurses, registrars, paediatricians, all on call or a few minutes away. And still they'd had their tragedies. With terrible ramifications.

'What if everyone is busy in Casualty and can't get away? What if two women come in at once?'

Misty had no such qualms. 'Then I manage with the woman's support person and phone for help if I need it.' Finally she gave him her attention. 'Didn't Andy explain the unit to you?'

No, and I'm far from comfortable, Ben thought, but he didn't say it because he'd only just got here and somehow he was still on the back foot with Misty. He hadn't figured how or why that had happened yet.

So instead he said, 'Andy hasn't really had the time. He said he'd deal with any problems but apparently problems are rare.'

Ben heard himself but he couldn't stop thinking

more negatively than he was speaking. He was a doctor. And a man. It was his job to fix things, and the concept that nothing was broken that required his skills was an interesting one to grapple with.

Misty was more than comfortable, he could see that, and he realised suddenly that he envied her.

'Problems are rare,' she said, 'because with well women and well babies, birth is a natural event, not an illness. We handle trouble efficiently if it happens. This is woman-centred care—so guess who the most important person is?'

He could hear the challenge in her voice and he didn't like the inference he'd disagree. Despite the fact he'd just pondered it himself. 'Why would you think I would have a problem with the woman being that?'

'It's been my experience with obstetricians. They like to know what's going on inside the woman, as if the exact progress and descent and dilation should be monitored for safe outcome. They think the more machinery the better.'

She looked up at him and raised her eyebrows. 'True?'

He shrugged, unwilling to get into another argument. Misty had no such qualms. He could tell she was fiercely protective about the way they worked at the lake.

'To a real birth attendant,' she said, 'a woman shows in her behaviour how her labour is progressing.'

Ben frowned. 'Not all the time. We've all seen

quiet achievers, and I think that generalised statement about obstetricians is unfair.' He added quietly, 'And this aggression doesn't seem like the woman I met last month.'

He heard her sigh and she ran a hand over her eyes and suddenly she looked less assured. He realised she was probably more tense than usual because he was there. He was sorry for that. He should have at least warned her he was coming, now that he thought about it.

'You're right,' she said. 'It was a generalisation. I apologise. I guess I'm still a little shocked to see you.'

Of course she was. And how typical of the Misty he did remember not to have a problem saying she was in the wrong. And he hadn't even mentioned he'd brought his daughter.

She turned away from him. 'But I do have work to do.'

'I'll help,' he said, and she paused as if she was going to say something then changed her mind. 'Fine' was all she said, so he followed her while she cleaned her trolley and washed instruments.

She had the delightful stride of a woman on a mission and he could have watched her all day.

Gloves were donned as she checked the placenta to ensure all of the lobes were present and accounted for, and he realised he'd forgotten that someone else ensured all this happened behind the scenes, because a missing lobe of placenta could indicate a high risk of bleeding for the woman so the carer needed to know.

He watched her examine the cross-section of umbilical cord to check there were two arteries and a vein. If only one artery instead of the usual two was present then the baby had an increased risk of kidney problems.

This was like a refresher at uni, only the lecturer looked nothing like the prune he'd had for anatomy.

Misty went back into the birth room and stripped the bed, and he helped her. Not something he usually did for the midwife, but Misty didn't seem to think it was a strange thing for him to do.

Ben looked around. These were all new experiences and he was actually enjoying himself. 'Where's our new baby?'

Misty looked across the room at the closed bathroom door and smiled at Ben's use of the possessive adjective. 'In the shower with Mum and Dad.'

Ben blinked. 'All three of them?'

'It's a big shower with two water roses.' Misty grinned at the disbelief in his voice and he tried to sound less stressed. He told himself that if he'd arrived this afternoon instead of now, then nothing would be different, except that he wouldn't have known how laid back it was here.

His brain chanted about infant hypoglycaemia from thermal stress. 'Won't the baby get cold?' He thought he sounded quite upbeat for that one.

She didn't quite say he was a panic merchant but the inference came through this time in her tone. 'Of course she won't. Where were you when skin-to-skin contact for the first hour of life came in? She'll be warmer against their skin than wrapped up in blankets. That's for sure.'

He sighed. Maybe it was just him. 'I've been out of obstetrics for too long.'

Even that admission didn't win him any points. 'Ha,' she said, as if all her suspicions had been proved correct. 'That's what I mean. This isn't obstetrics. This is normal birth. Later this year we're hoping to extend to births at home for those who want it with our midwives.'

No way. Ben blinked. He'd never be involved in home births. 'That won't happen in a hospital system here.'

She put her hands on her hips, and it reminded him of the day they'd first met. The day she'd scolded him for being so flippant about his life.

Suddenly the running of this unit was infinitely less important than what he'd come there for, but she had the bit between her teeth and he doubted he could stop her even if he wanted to.

It was amusing really how differently this woman affected him compared with anyone he'd ever known before. How she made him adjust his thinking, add shades of grey he'd never have considered because he valued her as a whole.

Even from the brief acquaintance they had he knew on some deep inner level that Misty would change his life for ever, even if only by passing through it.

And have a great effect on his daughter he hoped. No doubt she'd have them both fully educated before the end of Tammy's pregnancy.

'Wrong,' she said, and he remembered he was to be lectured. Actually, he wanted to kiss her.

'Home birth already happens in two health services that I know of. Montana and I have a friend, Mia, coming from Westside to run that side of it.'

He nodded because he'd better look like he was listening when all he could think about was how wonderful she'd tasted the last time he'd kissed her.

'And why not?' she said. 'Statistics prove the less intervention the better the outcome. Home birth is the norm in many countries.'

Ben rubbed his forehead. It would be best if he took his libido for a walk and came back later. 'I'd better go and see what's happening in Casualty. Andy said he'd meet me over there if I arrived early.'

He'd planned to broach the subject of why he was there but he was beginning to think she was deliberately directing the conversation to contentious issues between them.

His brow furrowed. Now, why would she do that? Maybe she wasn't as transparent as he liked to think she was. What was she afraid of?

Misty stopped and looked at him. 'Oh. OK.' She even looked slightly shamefaced at her fervour.

What if she was just as terrified as he was at them meeting again? He felt like slapping himself on the forehead. Of course she was. He'd been so surprised at how glad he was to see her that he hadn't allowed himself to notice before. 'I think what you do here is amazing, Misty. I'm sorry I didn't get it more quickly.'

Of course she'd need more time to acclimatise to him being there, and he needed to clarify the real reason he was there. Tammy was his reason. Maybe they both needed that clarified.

'I'll catch you later,' he said, and as he turned to leave he couldn't resist turning back one last time. 'It's really good to see you again, Misty.' Then he forced himself to walk away.

Misty watched him go. She should say something. There was so much unsaid between them she didn't know where to start, and she'd been gabbling about how great they were here because she'd wanted to fill the silences in case he asked her something she didn't want to answer.

But she could have done with a few answers herself. Like where he was living and when she could expect to see him next so she could prepare herself.

'It's nice to see you, too, Ben,' she whispered, but of course he didn't hear because he was long gone.

She'd bombarded him with zealous comments about the unit. Driving him away intentionally?

She thought about that explanation and maybe it was true because she really hadn't come to terms with his effect on her.

She sighed and glanced at the door to the birth suite. Here was something she did understand and feel comfortable with. 'You all OK in there?' Misty knocked on the bathroom door.

'Yep.' Ritchie sounded confident, finally. 'Did you want us to come out?'

'Only when you're ready. I'll go and make us all a cup of tea and some toast.'

Ben didn't know what he'd expected when he'd come to Lyrebird Lake. He'd thought more about Tammy's situation and seeing if the connection was still there with Misty, in that order, rather than work, but he'd always assumed he'd manage the work side.

It was certainly different to return to somewhere like this little casualty and birth centre. Apparently the hospital was growing busier now than it had been as more families moved into the lake area from the mine.

Andy said he'd spend most of his days seeing outpatients, ensuring the inpatients continued to improve, and be back-up for Maternity if any patients needed transfer to the base hospital.

Surprisingly, he had the feeling he was going to love the extra dimensions of the job. And despite the unusual first meeting this morning, the connection with Misty was still there—on his side anyway. But he needed to get over that.

He was there for Tammy, not for a relationship with Misty—not that she'd have him anyway. He was far too set in his insular lifestyle to appeal to a giving woman like her.

His priority should be to rebuild the relationship with his stepdaughter. Misty had been right in rejecting him at the beach. Her life held merit and direction and she didn't need him and his problems.

But in that first appraisal in the empty wing before the patient had come in, when Misty had looked up with such anxiety and even a flicker of fear of intruders, all he'd wanted to do had been to pull her into his arms and protect her. Even now he had to stop his feet from turning in her direction.

He'd have a talk to Andy about the safeguards if some crazy did go to Maternity looking for drugs or money. Misty, and the other women, of course, needed to be safe.

He found himself whistling. Something he hadn't done in years. It had been a great idea to come here.

He'd needed somewhere secure to take his daughter in this crisis while she was still reeling from the implications of her pregnancy.

He'd wondered, from the brief impression Misty had left him with, if Lyrebird Lake was the place that could help heal both of them from the damage Bridget and her mother had done.

* * *

By late that afternoon Cherry, Ritchie and baby Phoebe had gone home and the maternity unit was shut again.

Misty walked across the park and up the drive to the big old doctors' house that catered for visiting staff to the hospital. She'd moved in there when she'd started work, never having intended to stay with Montana and Andy, and she loved the relaxed feel of the old house.

The residence was run by Louisa, a round Yorkshire dumpling of a woman with merry eyes and big breasts, who'd hugged and kissed Misty's cheek at their initial meeting, and loved to spoil her.

Ned, the other resident, while supposedly semi-retired as a GP, was a busy little Scotsman who ran a clinic every afternoon in a rundown set of consulting rooms at the end of the house.

He hobbled a little with his stiff hip, and he and Louisa were an 'item'.

'Good afternoon, Ned.' Misty smiled at the elderly gentleman as she arrived home.

'Hello, there, Misty. So we've another change to the house.' Ned sat on the veranda that faced the hospital and carved a fat wombat out of driftwood with more gusto than artistry.

Misty's stomach took a dive. She'd almost convinced herself Ben would stay at the upmarket guest house on the lake but, of course, he was staying here! Murphy's law. She plastered a smile on her face. 'Dr Moore. Yes, I've met him.'

'He says you've more than met him,' Ned said archly, and Misty felt her face flame. Surely not.

'You're blushing, missy.' Ned chuckled. 'No need to be embarrassed about saving someone's life.'

Misty only just stopped herself from saying, *Oh, that*. Instead, she looked away at the distant hospital and said, 'I don't like to think about it, that's all.'

'Fair enough.' Ned nodded sagely. 'So we've a couple of new boarders.'

'A couple?' Misty stopped as she reached for the screen door handle.

'The new doctor and his daughter. Didn't you know about her?' Ned returned to his carving. 'About sixteen, lots of attitude and pregnant. Reminds me of my son when he was a teen and his girlfriend was pregnant. We fell out when he went into the army.'

Ned had a son? More importantly, Ben had a daughter and she was pregnant. Here was a whole world she didn't know about. The teenage daughter of the man whose life she'd saved and whose arms she'd slept in.

Ben wasn't here to see her at all. Just the place she'd told him about. Cold disappointment settled on her stomach.

That put a whole new slant on things and, really, it gave her the excuse she'd needed to shut down that attraction she'd been fighting this morning.

She thought about it some more. So despite the fact he'd infuriated her with his closed mind in the birth centre he'd actually come to take advantage of it.

Knowing that still didn't make it any easier. How was she going to face Ben's daughter when she had problems facing Ben? She sighed and opened the door. With her chin up, she guessed. That was all she could do.

Ben's entry into her life had certainly provided a whole host of new situations to cringe about, not least that she'd assumed he'd felt the same attraction she had.

She squeezed her eyes shut and then opened one to peer at Ned. 'Are they both here now?'

'Aye.' Ned nodded sagely as he whittled at his wombat's legs. 'The wee one is in the kitchen with Louisa and Ben.'

The 'wee one' was almost six feet tall and towered over Misty when she went in to meet her. Misty didn't look at Ben. She couldn't.

'Ah, here's Misty,' Louisa said placidly. 'This is Tammy, Dr Moore's daughter, and you've met Ben.'

The first thing about Tammy, apart from her height, was her magnificent blue eyes, just like Ben's. She needed to stop thinking about Ben's eyes. She concentrated on the daughter she hadn't known about and her mouth followed her brain, unfortunately.

'Hello, there, Tammy. You have your father's eyes.'

The girl tugged at the hem of the bulky sweater, unusual in the Queensland heat and obviously worn to disguise her pregnancy. She sniffed. 'He's not my real father, just my stepfather.'

Ben said, 'Tammy!' and Misty opened and shut her mouth but before she or Ben could think of anything to say, dear, sweet, unflappable Louisa had the situation under control.

'Put down your tail, young woman,' Louisa said calmly. 'Misty is the person you'll be needing in a while when that babe of yours comes along.'

Misty smiled at Louisa for bringing the whole situation back onto even ground. Then she smiled at Tammy again. 'You'll be fine. Welcome anyway, Tammy. I hope you'll settle in easily here.'

She glanced at Ben, who was clearly unhappy with his 'daughter', and she began to wonder at their relationship before she stopped herself.

It was all too complicated and none of her business. Instead, she stepped across to hug Louisa. 'And how are you?'

Louisa patted her arm. 'I'm fine. You know I love guests. Now, you scoot along and get changed and Tammy can set the table while you're gone. Ben will pour a glass of wine for you on the back veranda.'

Louisa knew how to organise people. That was one of the first things Misty had discovered when she'd moved into the residence and one of the most endearing.

She scooted and while she showered and changed she remembered the look of hurt on Ben's face at Tammy's disclosure. More things she didn't understand about Ben and maybe more reasons why she should tell herself she'd done the right thing a month ago.

Tammy was Ben's stepdaughter. So who had been looking after her while Ben had lived at his beach house? It had been hard to discern just how pregnant Tammy was, with the sweater she'd been wearing, so that gave no clues on how long they were staying.

Ben's house hadn't shown touches of a young girl, except suddenly Misty remembered the shells on the bathroom mirror, and nodded to herself.

There was no doubt Tammy's pregnancy was the real reason for Ben coming there.

CHAPTER SEVEN

THE sun was setting below the mountains behind the lake when Misty stepped out onto the back veranda.

She'd grown to love the view across the lake. The trees around the shore were reflected in the stillness of the water so they looked twice as tall as they were mirrored.

Tiny canoes and kayaks zigzagged across the water, disturbing flocks of waterbirds.

Every afternoon at sunset a new array of colours would transform the sky.

Ben was seated on the swing chair, swaying back and forwards as if unable to keep still, and he stood up as she closed the door behind her.

The lake faded into the distance and suddenly all she could see was him.

Big, dark, brooding. And not here at Lyrebird Lake for her at all.

His gaze drifted appreciatively over her T-shirt and jeans and something she'd randomly chosen was suddenly a satisfying choice. Funny how an attractive man could make you feel that way just by looking at you, she thought wryly.

Then he stood up, tall and magnetic in front of her. 'Here. Have this seat.

'The view's very pleasant,' he said, but the glint in his eye suggested he wasn't talking about the lake, and she felt that warmth of pleasure again. She really had to stop reacting to him.

'Thank you.' She sat down against her better judgement, it would have been churlish to refuse, but she unobtrusively crossed her fingers that he wouldn't end up hip to hip with her because she didn't think she could cope with that much proximity.

She knew where proximity with Ben could lead. 'The lake is lovely, isn't it?' How long could they chat about nothing before one of them fell asleep? she mockingly asked herself.

Thankfully he didn't sit next to her on the swing, but he was still too close when he pulled the chair up next to her and sat down.

'Different from the ocean,' Ben said in the same vein, but he was looking at her.

Ben tired of scenery talk first. 'I've thought about you a lot, Misty.'

She mentally sniffed. Ah, Ben, have you? I find that hard to believe. You haven't rung, you obviously figured out where to find me, and it's been a month. But she didn't say any of it.

FREE BOOKS OFFER

To get you started, we'll send you
2 FREE books and a FREE gift

- -

There's no catch, everything is **FREE**

Accepting your 2 **FREE** books and **FREE** mystery gift
places you under no obligation to buy anything.

Be part of the Mills & Boon® Book Club™ and receive your favourite
Series books up to 2 months before they are in the shops and delivered
straight to your door. Plus, enjoy a wide range of **EXCLUSIVE** benefits!

- Best new women's fiction – delivered right to
  your door with FREE P&P

- Avoid disappointment – get your books up to
  2 months before they are in the shops

- No contract – no obligation to buy

We hope that after receiving your free books you'll
want to remain a member. But the choice is yours.
So why not give us a go? You'll be glad you did!

Visit **millsandboon.co.uk** to stay up to date
with offers and to sign-up for our newsletter

2 **FREE** books
and a
FREE gift

M9EI

rs/Miss/Ms/Mr   Initials

BLOCK CAPITALS PLEASE

urname

ddress

Postcode

mail

MILLS & BOON®

Pure reading pleasure

ffer valid in the U.K. only and is not available to current Mills & Boon® Book Club™ subscribers to this series. Overseas and Eire please write for details. We reserve the
ght to refuse an application and applicants must be aged 18 years or over. Only one application per household. Offer expires 31st July 2009. Terms and prices subject to
ange without notice. As a result of this application you may receive further offers from other carefully selected companies. If you do not wish to share in this opportunity
ease write to the Data Manager at the address shown overleaf.

ills & Boon® Book Club™ is being used as a trademark.

NO STAMP NEEDED!

⊙ MILLS & BOON®
Book Club
FREE BOOK OFFER
FREEPOST CN81
CROYDON
CR9 3WZ

NO STAMP
NECESSARY
IF POSTED IN
THE U.K. OR N.I.

She should have but instead she looked away from him to the colours in the sky. He wasn't there for her. 'How? You don't know anything about me.'

'I'd like to think that isn't true.'

If he'd stretched out his hand he could have put his fingers over hers. He didn't, but just the thought of that possible contact had her sliding her hand unobtrusively under the back of her leg and out of reach.

Ben saw, grimaced, didn't comment, and went on softly, 'Actually, I think we learnt a lot about each other in a very short time. It's the present that's important.'

Well, she certainly had some blanks in his past. 'Do you have any more children?' she asked dryly.

As soon as the words left her mouth she felt ashamed. It really was none of her business. She'd been a stranger and he hadn't needed to tell her anything.

He handed her the wine and she knew she wouldn't drink it because if she couldn't keep control of her mouth without alcohol, the last thing she needed was to blurt out something she'd really regret.

'Thank you,' she said, and rested the glass on the table beside her. Frustratingly, she couldn't help it that her fingers shook.

Of course he didn't miss it. The way he was looking at her he wouldn't miss anything. 'What's wrong?'

'Nothing.' She looked away and then back at him. 'Though it is a little embarrassing to be talking to you here.'

He raised his eyebrows. 'Why? I thought we communicated very well the first time we met.'

She looked away and her voice dropped. 'We didn't communicate, Ben, we kissed, and if I hadn't left when I did we would have slept together in the other sense of the word.'

'But you did leave and still you made a big impact on me. That's why I'm here, Misty. But the last thing I want is to embarrass you.'

She wanted to ask, Is that the first or the second reason you're here, Ben? But she hoped she wasn't so pathetically needy.

Instead, she said brightly, 'So how long are you staying? It's certainly good timing for Andy and Montana.'

Ben sighed at her change of tack and she cringed a little at her own cowardice because he'd been brave to talk of the attraction between them, so why couldn't she be?

To make it worse, he allowed himself to be diverted and contrarily she didn't want that either.

He answered her second comment first. 'It's good timing for Tammy, too. Her school has suspended her and Bridget's mother disowned her when she found out she was pregnant. I've wanted to get Tammy away from both for a while now.'

She was glad she could be of some use, she thought, forcing herself to be realistic. 'So you think Lyrebird Lake will be good for your stepdaughter?'

'I do. But I should say I refuse to call Tammy my stepdaughter because until my wife's death I'd never suspected she wasn't my own.'

Misty's voice softened. Poor Ben. 'That must have been a shock.'

He shrugged but couldn't quite hide the impact it had on him. 'It took away any chance of my input over her life in her grandmother's care. All I can hope is that Tammy does understand that I still love her as my daughter. She's been mine since she was born. First steps, first words, first day at school—you can't erase parenting with a DNA test result.'

Ben stood up as if he didn't know what he could do. 'Lyrebird Lake can't be bad.' He turned to face her. 'Andy told me there's another young woman a little older than Tammy, with a two-year-old, who runs a young mums' class. I heard you were involved in that, too.'

'That's right.' He'd done his homework, Misty had to admit. 'Emma is great. I'd be happy to intro- duce the two girls if they agree. Emma's started uni part time to be a midwife.'

They were talking about something that had nothing to do with the issues between them and it was her fault. She'd changed the subject when she'd thought he would persist about the last time they'd met.

She wondered what she did want from this man she had nothing in common with except chemistry. What was realistic?

'So how long are you staying, Ben?' That was what she wanted to know. Needed to know. To work out how she was going to approach managing the way this man made her feel.

Ben gazed out over the lake. 'I expect to stay at the very least a month, with an option to extend after that. Tammy's baby is due in four weeks.'

A month or more. Her stomach fluttered with the news. How was she going to cope with that?

'Only a month to go,' she said with a bright smile plastered on her face. 'Same time as Montana? Goodness.' She sounded like a simpleton but Misty's mind spun with times and dates. 'Tammy's that close? I could hardly tell she was pregnant.'

Misty took a sip of the wine because she couldn't possibly get more addlebrained. Luckily Ben was thinking about his daughter and not the ditsy redhead opposite him.

'It's not a big baby,' Ben went on, oblivious to Misty's squirming. 'She hides her bump in those heavy jumpers no matter what the weather and hasn't been eating well.'

Misty could see his concern and gratefully she allowed herself to be drawn away from her own worries. 'Queensland's heat will make camouflage a bit trickier. I think the sooner we get her and Emma together the better.'

She thought back to his reactions this morning in

the unit. 'So how do you feel about having your step-grandchild born in a birth centre?'

He looked away to the view and she wondered why. 'You said it was the best,' he said. 'That's why we're here.'

He managed to hide what he was thinking much more successfully than she could. 'Lyrebird Lake is the best,' she agreed, 'but you haven't answered my question.'

He smiled ruefully. 'How do I feel?' He shrugged. 'I'm worried.'

Ah. No surprise there. 'Why?'

'Mainly because I fear she won't be able to cope with the pain of contractions, not having the option of an epidural or strong drugs, and I won't be able to help her once she's in labour in this environment.'

At least he was being honest, Misty acknowledged that, but he just didn't get it. It wasn't his fault. It was his training in the big hospital system. 'She could transfer out. But is she the one that won't cope or is it you, Ben?'

He shrugged, and she could see he wasn't willing to go there. 'It's not just the labour. I'm worried that she'll get sick, worried that she'll get postnatal depression because her mother did, with tragic consequences. Tammy is high risk.'

Ben definitely had demons and she couldn't fix them.

'All women are at risk, Ben, and maybe there is

more risk for Tammy, but that can be monitored. Physically she's a normal teenager. Younger women than Tammy have been having babies in other cultures since the beginning of time.'

'But not my daughter.' The anguish was real in his voice and she wanted to hug him and tell him Tammy would be OK. Tammy's mother's history of depression was a real concern, of course. But birth outside the medical model was something her brother, Andy, had had to come to grips with for Montana, and Ben needed to as well.

She didn't know what she could say to help him. 'I'm sure you said you wrote a book on postnatal depression, that makes you an expert, so you should have that covered. Tell me, Ben, are there any good feelings about this pregnancy in your head?'

He frowned. 'Of course there are—or will be when she's safely delivered.'

She'd known it. Misty smiled at Ben. 'She won't be "delivered" if she has her baby here, Ben. She'll give birth and we'll support her.' Misty couldn't help rubbing it in and reluctantly he smiled.

'OK.' He held up his hands in surrender. 'Women-centred care—non-intervention, not "delivery". I can feel the grey hairs already. And that's not counting trying to be a parent to a teenage girl I really do need help with.'

That was what he wanted from her. That was all. To help him, short term, to parent his teenage daughter and be there when she gave birth. It wasn't an onerous thought but it stung a little when it came with his connection to her.

Misty sighed and wispy dreams of Ben being irresistibly attracted to her dissolved into vapour. 'I understand a little of what she's feeling, Ben. My mother died when I was young and as a teen I was angry. That's when a young woman needs her mother—and again when she's pregnant. I understand her mother may not be alive but Tammy has you. She's not alone. Just like I have Andy, and now Montana.'

Ben searched her face as if to see if she really believed what she'd said. 'So you're saying I've done the right thing, bringing her here.'

Of course he had. *Her* issues with him being here were her own problem. 'I'm saying you're not alone in dealing with this if you don't want to be. You'll both be fine because the support network is here.'

She needed to get over feeling bitter that Ben hadn't followed her after all. He'd decided his daughter could benefit from the service Misty had told him about. That was a good thing.

She'd make a real effort to help Tammy settle because that was why Ben was there and she needed to accept that as soon as possible before she said or did something rash.

Then Ben blew all her good sense out of the water. 'I do feel good about being here.' His crooked smile tugged at her and she felt as if the air on the veranda had suddenly been sucked away to leave her gasping.

'I see they rent canoes on the lake,' he mused. 'Any chance you'll come for a paddle with me tomorrow afternoon and show me the sights?'

No. None. She shook her head. 'What about Tammy?'

'I asked her.' He grinned at Misty like a mischievous boy and she found herself returning the smile. 'She told me she was too fat and to take a jump.'

Ben's glance passed over her in the way men seemed to learn from birth. It really wasn't fair, and the effect he had on her brought back all the weaknesses she'd tried to deny at the beach. This was not a good idea.

'Come with me,' he said. 'It'll be fun.'

What mischief could they get up to in a canoe? Misty told herself, and then the picture of herself in Ben's arms as they drifted past the tree-lined banks left her in no doubt that mischief could be had.

Misty fought valiantly and unsuccessfully not to blush. She stood up and went to the rail to at least hide the evidence.

'We'll see. It depends on what time I get off work.'

'And on the weather, and that all the boats aren't rented out, and that neither of us breaks a leg.' Ben teased as he came to stand beside her. 'Are you frightened of me, Misty?'

Misty turned to face him and she searched his

strong features for the understanding he'd surprised her with before. 'No, Ben. Of me,' she said very quietly. He smiled at her. There it was. Understanding.

'Well, you should be.'

The next afternoon the sun shone warmly through the few scattered clouds in an otherwise blue Queensland sky and the lake looked extremely inviting to Ben as he walked beside Misty down to the boatshed. And not just the lake looked inviting.

'This is the first time I've been off work in the last month,' Misty mused.

'The babies understand you need to play sometimes. And the shed had plenty of boats.' Ben grinned down at the woman walking beside him and congratulated himself on a great idea. 'It's not even raining.'

'Meaning?' Misty looked up at him and he resisted the urge to drop a kiss on her lips. She really should be more wary of him than of herself. She had disgustingly strong willpower.

'Meaning divine intervention itself is not going to stop you from being alone in my company.'

Misty glanced around at the little boats dotted over the lake. 'I don't think being alone will be a problem, Ben,' she said dryly.

He deliberately misunderstood her. 'Good.'

She raised her eyebrows at his cheeky comment. 'Just don't try to save any birds and hit your head.'

'Ouch.' So she had a mean streak as well. He liked that. Ben started to whistle an Irish courting tune that had come from nowhere into his head and he looked down at the copper-headed woman beside him and smiled at the world.

A voice hailed them from the boatshed and old Clem, who Ben had met last night when he'd arranged this, came out, wiping varnish from his hands on a rag.

Clem looked at Misty. 'Howdy, Miss Buchanan.'

'Hello, Clem. How's the granddaughter?'

The old man's face creased into a road map of pride. 'Pretty as a picture and just as sweet.'

Misty nodded. 'I saw them at home yesterday and Ellie's a great little mother.'

'Take's after my sainted wife,' Clem said, and Misty looked at Ben.

'Clem's daughter, Ellie, had her first baby last week. I visit her on the early discharge programme we have.'

Clem nodded. 'It was a real boost to this place when Miss Buchanan's brother came here, then his wife and now his sister. Now look what we got. My girl didn't have to go to a place where she didn't know anyone to have the babe.'

He shook his grizzled head and Ben began to see that what he had considered a quaint service could, in fact, be something to be very proud of.

He reminded himself to talk to Andy when he had a chance to find out how it had all begun.

'Anyway, come for the boats, have you, Doc?'
Clem pointed with the rag at two canoes tied up at
the end of the jetty. 'Just leave 'em there when you're
finished and I'll put 'em away,' he said. 'Enjoy.'

'Thank you,' Ben said, and he reached forward
and shook the old man's gnarled hand. The smell of
turpentine would follow them for the evening but he
could live with that. He was sure Misty could too.

Five minutes later they drew away from the jetty
and, of course, the superior edge from his prestigious
boarding-school training proved no match for
Misty's obvious aquatic skills. 'So you can swim,
surf, and canoe with consummate ease?'

'Another blow for male domination,' she teased
him back, and he had to laugh at his own wounded
pride as she paddled away from him.

He dug his paddle in and chased. There was no
doubt she was a strong purgative for his arrogant soul.

'Andy and I grew up on the water at Bundeena,'
she called over her shoulder.

He finally caught up and they both stopped
paddling and just drifted over the clear water.

She turned to face him and the little spots of
colour and the excitement in her eyes made her look
even more beautiful to him. 'Bundeena is an inlet on
the south side of Port Hacking and is surrounded by
national park. Lots of outdoor stuff happens there.'

'It sounds beautiful.'

Misty laughed. 'I had great friends but used to

think it was a hole. No nightclubs, or pubs—just a club for the oldies and good, clean fun for the kids.'

Her face saddened. 'When Mum died we had to move out west of Sydney and Andy commuted to med school. Eventually I finished school and did my nursing degree. That's where I met Montana and Mia.'

She glanced around at the lake and the other craft in the distance. 'I think that's why Andy likes it here. Because of the water.'

I like it here because of you, Ben thought, but he didn't say it. He wasn't sure that he wanted to put that much pressure on himself. He had the feeling she wasn't ready to hear it either.

'What happened to your dad?' he said instead.

'He died when I was about five. I don't remember much about him except he used to laugh a lot.' She looked at him. 'But enough about me. Tell me something about your life, Ben Moore. What makes you tick?'

Ben wasn't sure that he did tick. He'd been dead for years until this little spitfire had come along. She tilted her face at him and dared him with her eyes to open up to her but he couldn't do it. Wouldn't do it!

Typically, he changed the subject. 'I thrive on competition.' The willow trees along the bank looked far enough away for her to forget the topic. 'Race you to the shore.'

'If I win, you tell me something,' Miss I-will-not-be-diverted said, and he nodded. But he'd win.

Of course he didn't. He led for most of the way but at the end her lighter kayak wiggled its stern at him as she paddled past ten metres from the shore.

She dug her paddle into the water to skid to a stop in the shallows, facing him, and Ben threw up his hands in disgust.

He had to laugh. 'That will not happen again. I'll be out here every afternoon, practicing, because it's very bad for my morale to lose to a mere woman.'

'Poor Ben,' she teased, and stepped lightly—not as easy as it looked he found out himself—out of her boat and onto the bank. 'Drag your boat up here and I'll pat your back.'

There were some things a man couldn't bear and perky little smart Alecs with attitude needed to be taught a lesson.

He followed her up the bank and under the trees and suddenly they were in a different place. The hillside angled away from them rock strewn and scrubby, but under the trees the lake lapped the shore and it was cool and dimly lit and delightfully secluded.

Misty stopped as if she'd just realised their isolation, and Ben planted his feet and smiled. 'Now, this is nice,' he said.

Misty brushed her hair from her face with her finger and faced him. He saw her notice the backpack and she changed the subject with barely hidden relief. 'I meant to ask earlier. What did you bring in your bag?'

So she didn't want to be kissed. Sensible girl. He'd called her that before, he remembered. He damped down the urges that clamoured for attention and lifted the bag from his shoulder.

'Aha. Curiosity.' He bent down and unzipped it and looked inside. 'Actually, it's pretty boring. I'd like one of those Mary Poppins travel bags that everything comes out of. You know chairs, table, lampshade…'

She blinked in surprise at his off-the-cuff comment and he supposed it must be a bit strange for a bloke to wish for the world's most famous nanny's accessories.

He guessed it was a little embarrassing. 'Tammy loved the DVD. I've watched it a hundred times with her. I used to do the Dick Van Dyke impersonations, and she'd laugh.' He looked away. Actually, they had been some of the many good times he could remember. Poor Tammy.

Misty didn't doubt he cursed himself for giving away even that much so she didn't comment on his obvious regrets. But it was nice to get at least a tiny glimpse of what he'd been like as a father. 'Maybe you could try and remember some skits for when she's in labour.'

They smiled at each other. Humour in the birth unit was rarely appreciated by the woman in labour, and they both knew it.

'Hmm. That would go down well,' Ben said.

'She's sixteen. Apparently I'm not going anywhere near her until after the baby is born.'

'She told you that?'

'Yeah. But that's fine. I'll be a mess anyway and probably wouldn't be any help to her.'

'Poor midwife, having you in the background.'

'Poor you.'

'Yeah. Poor me.' They smiled at each other again and the mood shifted.

Without taking his eyes off her, Ben reached into the bag and pulled out a folded rug. He knelt down and unfolded it over the scratchy grass.

'Would you like to sit down?' he said, and Misty felt the flutter in her stomach respond to the invitation in his voice and eyes.

Automatically she straightened her own side of the mat until it lay between them like a tartan square of no-man's-land that she wasn't sure she was game to edge onto.

Ben just smiled at her hesitation and stretched himself out one side. He pulled the bag across and produced a drink. 'If you sit next to me I'll give you a mango juice. I know you like it.'

Misty had to smile. So he'd remembered that from the beach, had he? 'I didn't drink it last time.'

'And very sensible you were, but it's hotter today and you must be parched from beating me in a kayak.'

'You shouldn't be the one to sound smug.'

'Smug?' She watched him mull over the word and

then nod his head. 'Yep.' He nodded again with conviction. 'As the only person here with cold juice to offer, I am smug.'

'As the outright winner, I, too, am smug. Therefore I will accept one, thank you.'

She eased onto the mat next to him and took the bottle. The brush of his fingers made her pulse rate increase and she looked away. This was not a good idea.

When she opened the lid of the bottle, the cracking sound of the broken seal seemed to echo around her.

Why did her senses seem to become so much more receptive when she was near Ben?

They both gazed out onto the lake through the fronds of the overhanging trees and the sun glinted off the water, the juice was icy cold and fruity, and the company was... She took a sip and when she turned back to face him he was watching her mouth.

'You've got your own. Don't look at mine.'

He looked down at the juice in his hand as if he'd forgotten it was there. He cracked the lid and looked down at it. 'Noisy little blighters,' he said. 'Yours looks better,' he said with a slight smile, and then he seemed to finally relax.

She wondered if he could feel those tiny eddies of breeze that seemed to be tickling her skin or maybe his skin wasn't a mass of raw nerve endings like hers had suddenly become.

The silence stretched. 'I was surprised to see you

live at the residence. I thought you and Tammy might move into the big guesthouse.'

Ben looked across the water at the tall white building to the left. 'I was going to but Andy suggested Louisa and Ned might be better company for Tammy when I was called out at night.'

He looked back at her and smiled. 'He did mention his sister was a midwife and stayed there, too.'

So Ben had known Misty would be under the same roof before he'd arrived. It would have been nice to have had that advantage. Never mind. She'd managed very well considering the lack of warning.

A rustle from the bushes behind them made them both turn and from the thicker foliage came the identical sound of the mango-juice lid opening. Then the noise came again twice more in quick succession.

Ben blinked and Misty smiled in sudden comprehension. Montana had told her about this.

'Lyrebird,' Misty breathed almost inaudibly.

A small brown bird poked his head out of the bush and stared beadily at them.

When they didn't move he stepped out fastidiously as if to avoid soiling his feet and lifted the heavy tail that he dragged behind him. Fan shaped and grey-brown, his tail shimmied at them in a ruffle of feathers as he turned full circle, balancing the extra weight with some effort. The bird gave two more renditions of the juice-opening noise and then dropped his tail and disappeared back into the bush as if he'd done his job and was now off duty.

Ben let go of the breath he hadn't realised he'd held. He felt suddenly lighter than he had for a long time, no doubt from the euphoria of hypoxia when he had failed to breathe, but nonetheless it was a good feeling.

He turned to look at Misty and she smiled back at him, his own pleasure reflected in her green eyes.

'That was pretty special,' Ben said. He leaned across and took Misty's hand in his and pulled her across to him until he could put his arm around her.

'Mmm-hmm,' Misty said as she leaned against him and closed her eyes to replay the sight in her mind.

He stared at her now familiar features as she breathed gently beside him, eyes shut, relaxed and enjoying the serenity around them.

Peace seemed to steal into his bones, dissolving some of the pain and guilt he'd held buried for so long.

Misty felt warm and wonderful under his arm but there was no rush to alter the mood because he could just turn his face and look out over Lyrebird Lake and thank his lucky stars he'd come there.

For the moment, and for today, that was enough.

CHAPTER EIGHT

THE next evening when Tammy joined them on the veranda Misty moved over to encourage the young woman to sit next to her.

'We get the swing, Tammy. Men not allowed. Are you a swinger or a sitter?'

Tammy plonked down next to Misty and stared at the ground. 'Swinging makes me sick when I'm pregnant.'

'I'm not a fan of the vigorous rock.' She glanced at Ben. 'If you sit here with a man he has to make it swing. It's in their make-up.'

'Dad, I mean, Ben,' she corrected herself, 'used to take me to the park when I was a kid, but that stopped when he left Mum.'

'You liked the swings then. I had fun at the park with you,' Ben said quietly. 'It was peaceful and those times are some of my most treasured memories.'

Tammy smiled and said dryly in a voice beyond

her years, 'Nobody was yelling at the park. Mum loved a good yell.'

Ben shrugged apologetically. 'Your mum and I weren't terrific together. I thought I was making her even more unhappy.'

'She really wasn't terrific with anyone, but she got worse when you left.' Tammy glanced at Misty. 'He left my mum the day after I turned twelve. Mum died three months later.'

The flatness of her tone spoke volumes. 'You shouldn't have left me with her.'

Misty didn't know where to look or how to help. These people had huge issues beyond her simple solutions. She wondered if she should get up and leave but Ben must have sensed her intention.

He lifted his hand in her direction. 'Stay, Misty. Please. If you weren't here we probably wouldn't be talking about something we should have talked about years ago.'

Ben edged forward in his seat to catch his daughter's eye. 'You know why I left you both, Tammy.'

Tammy refused to look at him. 'Because you wanted to do your own thing and I wasn't important enough to stay.'

Ben shook his head. 'Because I could see what the fighting was doing to you. To all of us.'

Now she looked at him but it was more of a glare. 'She put me in a boarding school. How was that better?'

Ben sighed. 'Your mother told me she denied me

shared custody because I worked such long hours, and I did then, but we had some good times on your leave weekends.'

'We did until Mum died.'

'It was your choice to stop. I'm sorry, Tammy. I know it's been hard for you but we've got a chance to spend some time together here. Now.' He stared at his daughter's face. 'Let's do that.'

'OK,' Tammy said, but even Misty could hear the lack of belief in the word and she hoped Ben meant what he said because Tammy certainly needed the attention.

The next night Ben and Tammy went out for dinner. His daughter might have been in a better mood if she hadn't been asked after Misty had. Misty had declined Ben's invitation and unfortunately Tammy had overheard, and the evening wasn't the complete success Ben had hoped for.

He just didn't get it and Misty resolved to hand out a few hints when she had him to herself.

The next morning Tammy waylaid Misty in the hallway to hand out a few hints of her own.

'Can I talk to you for a minute?' She avoided Misty's eyes as she indicated with her hand the doorway into her room.

Misty allowed herself to be ushered into Tammy's bedroom and glanced around for somewhere to perch.

There really wasn't a surface, including the carpet, unlittered with clothes, which made it difficult to decide where to sit. How could such a mess have happened in so few days?

Tammy solved the problem by sweeping the only bundle of clean clothes from the desk chair onto the floor.

Misty blinked and couldn't help herself. 'I'll bet you didn't fold those,' she said dryly, and Tammy looked up in confusion.

Tammy looked down at the pile tipped on its side, and shrugged. 'Why would I?'

'Because Louisa isn't your slave, is four times your age and deserves a little respect for the help she's offering.'

She looked at Tammy and smiled. 'But I'm not your mother or your father so go ahead. You wanted to say something to me?'

Tammy glanced around at the mess in the room and frowned. 'You know, you're right.' She looked at Misty and sighed. 'I've been feeling sorry for myself, which only makes me worse.' She kicked the nearest article of clothing. 'I couldn't do this at boarding school but my grandmother didn't expect me to do anything in her house.'

Tammy picked up the clothes she'd just knocked over and put them back on the desk. 'I'll fix it. I do like Louisa.'

'Wow.' Misty was seriously surprised and impressed. She looked at the young girl in front of her and smiled. 'It's pretty brave to admit that. If you want to do it now, I'll help you and we'll have it done in no time. Then we can have breakfast together.'

Tammy looked up as if assessing if Misty meant it. 'If you want.'

They sorted the room quickly and Tammy even giggled at Misty's amazement when she saw Tammy's tiny underwear.

'So you actually wear G-strings and find them comfortable?'

'Yeah.' But her tone said, Of course! 'I've even got G-string napkins for after the baby's born. I read about them in a magazine.'

'You learn something every day.' Misty shook her head and suddenly she saw just how lonely Tammy was. 'You said you wanted to talk about something?'

Tammy looked away. 'I wondered if you thought my dad was OK. He seems to like you.'

Misty could hear the subtle jealousy that Tammy tried to hide and she didn't blame her. She'd only just got her father back and here he was paying attention to someone else when she'd thought she'd have him all to herself.

Misty trod carefully. 'What's not to like? Did your dad tell you how we met?'

Tammy nodded. 'You saved him when he nearly drowned. I can't imagine my dad needing anyone like that, but I guess he would have died if you hadn't been there.'

Misty pushed away the images that rose. 'I don't like thinking about that but, yes, there was a big chance he could have.'

Tammy frowned as if the reality of it had only just occurred to her. 'I would have been an orphan.'

Misty smiled. 'I'm glad you're not.'

Tammy finally smiled back with a genuine smile. 'So am I. He's not perfect but, you know, neither am I.'

Misty picked up the last article of clothing off the floor. 'None of us are,' she said dryly. 'You know your dad wants to spend more time with you and get to know you again. He's just got to learn how.'

Tammy paused as she closed a drawer. 'Does he? Or does he want to get to know you more?'

Misty stared at the back of Tammy's head. 'Maybe he wants to know both of us. But you'll always be special to him because you're his daughter.'

Tammy turned to face her. 'But I'm not really, am I? And if I wasn't pregnant, I'd still be at school.'

Misty finally felt she could see Tammy's unhappiness. 'You can't wipe twelve years of parenting out with a blood test. Of course you're his daughter. I think he's secretly glad to have you to himself.' She looked around and realised they'd finished tidying up. 'Let's have something to eat before I have to go to work.'

Ben had left an hour ago. Louisa was missing in

action but the table was set and the breakfast room was empty except for them.

'What have you planned for today, Tammy?' Misty said, as she poured her juice. The young woman had pushed her sweater sleeves up her arms and already she was fiddling with the neckline because of the heat.

'Nothing.' Tammy grimaced. 'I hate this heat.'

Misty didn't comment on that yet! 'Well, so far I have no one in labour and we have a working bee happening at the unit today.'

Tammy didn't say anything and Misty went on, 'Some of the women from the community are coming and I've asked Emma to come in today to help me. Your dad mentioned Emma, didn't he? She's nineteen and her baby is two years old now.'

Misty waited but Tammy still didn't say anything. 'We're opening a day room, somewhere the women can sit, if they want to, and chat. It's a great opportunity for you and Emma to get to know each other better. Why don't you come and help?'

Tammy shrugged. 'What can I do to help? I'm pregnant.'

Misty glanced at Tammy's big belly. 'I can see that. It gets boring towards the end, doesn't it?'

Tammy pulled a face. 'You bet.'

'Well, because you're pregnant, you could give us ideas about what's comfortable and what's not. Your input into what you think would make pregnant

ladies feel better would be great. And you could meet
Emma's daughter, Grace, who's a real delight. Get
used to handling little children.'

Tammy looked up and finally a glimmer of
interest showed. Misty had hopes she was getting
through to her.

'The birth centre is where you'll have your baby
and it's always good to get to know the place, rather
than turning up in labour there for the first time.'

Tammy looked at Misty and then she frowned.
'Why are you being so kind to me?'

Misty buttered her toast. 'Can't I be? I thought I
was asking you to be kind to me.' She took a bite of
her toast and left Tammy to decide.

Tammy mulled it over and finally a shy smile
appeared. 'If you really think I could help?'

Misty nodded. 'I do. That's excellent. You're the
perfect person for the job. On one condition.'

Tammy's eyes narrowed as if she'd known it
was a trick. 'What?' Distrust was back in full force
in her voice.

Misty shrugged apologetically. 'You have to take
your jumper off. Honestly, you make me perspire just
looking at you.'

To Misty's relief Tammy laughed, and it was a
genuine one. 'OK. Gladly. I'm so over being hot.'

Tammy pulled the sweater over her head then and
there and she and Misty both giggled as she draped
it over a chair with a sigh of relief.

They both contemplated Tammy's stomach. 'You have a really neat tummy, you know.'

'Yeah. I'm getting used to it.'

An hour later at the centre, Misty looked at Montana, drinking tea at the desk, and the few chairs they had. There would be more women coming. The buzz of excitement promised a productive day.

Misty gazed at the small crowd. 'We may as well do a clinic while we're all here. I think I'll ring Sue and Sara and then they can ring other clients if they want to.'

She turned to Montana. 'It'll be great when we have a women's waiting area to use in early labour. They can relax and chat and it would give us somewhere to meet and we can all sit together.'

Montana nodded. 'Maybe we could hold the antenatal education there instead of the school hall. Make it child friendly.'

Misty thought of Ben and grinned. 'The Women Friendly Centre.'

Montana smiled and stood up. She rubbed her back. 'I need to walk. I'll pop over to Matron and see what else she has for us. There's furniture in storage from when we cleared this room that we could use, but I don't know how comfortable it is. The orderly and one of the gardeners would be happy to help move it.'

Misty could feel the excitement. This was a good idea.

Twenty minutes later Matron sent over two cleaning staff to help spruce the room and a water cooler she had in her office.

Louisa arrived and donated two squashy beanbag seats left by a past guest of the residence, plus a huge basket of fabric and threads and patchwork magazines.

Gradually there was purpose and comfort and direction in the room as the women began to plan quilts to cover lounges and use as throws.

Tammy started off keeping her distance but was soon found entertaining the toddlers that had begun to collect at their mothers' skirts.

When Emma arrived with her daughter the two young women drew together naturally, and Misty sighed with relief to see Tammy look even more comfortable.

Women brought cushions and plants, paintings, and rugs to throw over vinyl hospital lounge chairs. Children's toys arrived from the tiny old children's ward that had closed down and the hospital gardener brought two glorious tubs of petunias to put on a stand outside the window.

Suddenly it was a beautiful room, with women quietly quilting, and at one point Misty looked across and Tammy had Emma's Grace tucked into her shoulder asleep. The look of wonder on Tammy's face did more to reassure Misty that all would be well than anything else could have.

Tammy would be fine. By lunch the old annexe

had turned into a comfy day room and the hospital kitchen had sent up trays of sandwiches to accompany the tea Tammy and a couple of others began to make in potfuls.

On his lunch-break Ben walked into the new day room and saw what Misty and the women had achieved. Then he saw his daughter, smiling and at ease with other pregnant women, and saw that for the first time in public she had shed her heavy pullover and dressed in a spotted maternity blouse that made her look very young and pretty.

How had Misty achieved so much when he hadn't been able to? Ever since her mother's death he and Tammy hadn't regained their closeness. Not only did he feel he'd failed her mother but that he'd failed Tammy, too.

Now Misty was doing what he couldn't. Communicating with his daughter and bringing a smile to her face. She'd broken through Tammy's reserves. And his.

But after Tammy's baby was born they'd have to move on. What would happen then? The pressure would be on because he couldn't fail his grandchild as well.

Misty saw Ben hesitate at the door. She saw the way his eyes flickered over his daughter and the look of pain he tried to hide. What were his demons? She wished she knew because he should be counting his blessings, not rueing his past.

He looked up at her and smiled and his pleasure seemed to wrap around Misty like a hug. Suddenly he was the only person she could see in the room. Just a smile and he had her.

Ben crossed the room to her and took her hand in his. 'Thank you, Misty. It's great to see Tammy out of her jumper and looking so at ease.'

Misty looked across at his daughter. 'Tammy's been a wonderful help and has hit it off with Emma. I'm really pleased about that.'

Ben squeezed her hand once more and she looked down at their fingers, entwined in front of everyone in the room. She returned the pressure before she eased herself free.

'So am I,' Ben said. 'I really appreciate your help, Misty. I was at my wits' end.'

When Misty looked up she saw Tammy's face and the frozen look his daughter wore hinted that all the good work they'd achieved this morning had just been undone by Ben's attention to her.

Unintentional it may have been, but it was the last thing either of them would have wanted.

By three o'clock people started to drift away to gather children from school, but the sense of community from their achievement thrilled them immensely.

Tammy had returned to the residence not long after Ben's visit and Misty looked around at the almost empty room and realised that Montana was missing.

She circled the unit and finally found her friend staring out the window of the bedroom. 'Hello, there. You OK?'

Montana turned to face her. 'It's time. I think you need to call Andy. My contractions have started.'

Misty had wondered how she would feel at this moment, because Montana's last birth had been over in less than an hour and it was her job to keep her friend safe, but she felt calm and focussed, thankfully.

Montana was a month early but she'd been the same with Dawn. She would be fine but Andy had better get there quick. 'I'll ring him now.' She paused and looked back at her friend. 'Do you feel well?'

'Perfect. Excited but worried Andy won't get here. Tell him to hurry. Safely.'

Misty had checked Montana antenatally that morning and her baby had been positioned perfectly for birth, with a wonderfully reassuring heartbeat.

Misty picked up the Doppler for a quick listen and the baby's heartbeat filled the room until both women smiled at each other.

'Just to hear my baby makes me feel calmer,' Montana said, then she grimaced as the next contraction arrived. 'I'll stand in the shower while the bath fills up.'

'I'll ring Andy.' Misty went through the doorway and ran chest to chest into Ben, coming the other way.

'Whoa, there.' Ben put his arms up to stop her

falling and he couldn't help enjoying the firmness of her arms as he forced his hands to let go.

Memories rushed in to remind him how she would feel, could feel, if he could just get past the frustrating barriers she'd erected. His hands tingled and his brain felt fogged from just that contact. It was ridiculous what this woman did to him.

Her clear green eyes stared straight into his and her sharp words shattered his daydreams. 'I don't have time for this, Ben.'

Ben stepped back. 'Sorry.' He held up his hands as if to say, See, I let you go. 'I thought you'd fall. Where are you off to in such a hurry?'

'The phone.' Misty looked around him towards the desk. 'Montana's started labour and we need Andy back here.'

Andy's wife. He remembered the illogical fears he'd held when Bridget had gone in to have Tammy. Surely Andy would want him to be there until he came.

He'd met Montana again briefly at lunch in the midst of Misty's collection of ladies. A female gathering that had him beating a hasty retreat back to casualty, though it had been good to see Tammy so socially comfortable. He'd figured Misty wouldn't have time to talk to him then and hoped to catch a few minutes with her now. But that wasn't going to happen.

Mind on job, he warned himself.

CHAPTER NINE

'I HAVE to get back to Montana.' Misty stepped away.

'Of course,' he said. 'May I stay until Andy arrives? Where is she?'

Misty paused, surprised how glad she was that Ben would stay until Andy came. Everything would be fine but here was where it was tricky when you were close to someone you were looking after.

Just the reassurance that Ben offered as a very skilled professional took all the worry from her shoulders. She could handle most things but Ben was there for back-up for the unthinkable.

'That will be good. Thank you.' She spun on her heel and then looked back over her shoulder. 'Actually, you could ring Andy for me so that he knows Montana is in labour, and I'll go back to her.'

Now it was all about Montana and her baby and Andy. She was so fortunate to be here for their special event, Misty reminded herself as she knocked on the bathroom door.

Montana stood in the shower with her back against the wall, and the water streamed over her stomach as she breathed through a contraction.

Misty waited for her to drop her shoulders in a sigh and open her eyes.

'You can listen now. The pain's just finishing,' Montana said, and she twisted her body to face Misty so she could place the Doppler again to hear the baby.

The clop, clop of Montana's baby's heartbeat was clear and true. They listened for a minute and then the next pain began and Montana closed her eyes.

Misty stepped back to check the level of water and temperature in the big square bath.

She remembered Montana telling her of Andy's horror when the bath had been donated. He hadn't been thrilled when a grateful member of the town's only family of plumbers had installed it free of charge. Montana had been ecstatic.

Andy's reluctance at the thought of water births had diminished over time with the excellent results, and Montana had chosen this mode for her own birthing experience.

The bath was big, a four-person spa with no jets, and the temperature was set to suit the baby as he or she entered the world.

Misty slipped from the room and turned the volume up on the slow rhythmic music Montana had chosen for the birth.

'I don't know what to do in a water birth.' Ben's

voice came from behind her, quiet but with an unmistakable thread of uneasiness.

'You don't have to do anything.' She smiled at him. 'Though I admire your honesty. That must have been hard for you to admit,' she teased.

'Yes.' Ben smiled back.

'Montana will do it all. Since they installed the bath fifty per cent of all births are in here. It's hands off.'

'Oh, Lord.' Ben screwed his face up. 'I can see my learning curve is going to be huge here.'

Misty grinned at him. 'Andy's was. Keep having an open mind.'

He really was trying, Misty thought, and it took a big man to accept he had a lot to learn from people less medically qualified than he was. She was proud of him, which seemed a proprietorial thing to be when she thought about it. Her heart thumped. Best not to think about it.

Montana breathed quietly with her eyes closed and Misty drew Ben out of the room in case they disturbed her space.

At that moment Andy arrived, out of breath and quick to strip off his shirt and tie. His shoes and socks went one by one as he hopped on alternate legs towards the sink to wash his hands. Andy's head swivelled as he looked for his wife.

His brow creased. 'How is she? Where is she?' He had no time for pleasantries.

Misty felt the catch of tears in her throat as she

saw how concerned her big strong brother was for the most important person in his life. 'Montana's fine. In total control and in the shower. We've run the bath.'

Andy winced. 'Oh, goody.'

Misty grinned. 'You're outgunned, big brother.'

'Don't I know it.' He looked at Ben. 'Never fall in love or they change your world.'

Without waiting for an answer from Ben, Andy reached for the towel. 'Contractions?'

'Contractions started fifteen minutes ago. She'll be glad to see you. Foetal heart rate 140.'

'I'll leave you, then.' Ben's quiet voice made Andy pause.

Andy frowned. 'Stick around. Please. Don't go too far. I may have become more used to this over the last twelve months but this is *my* wife and child. You know how paranoid medical people are. It's nice to know you're here.'

Ben smiled. 'Of course. I'd be honoured.' He looked at Misty and she smiled, too.

'You'll get used to water births,' she said, and Ben just nodded, but deep inside he guaranteed he wouldn't. No way.

Andy opened the bathroom door and as he paused, Misty could almost see her brother's love pour across the room to wrap around his wife. Andy stripped off his belt and trousers and unselfconsciously, dressed only in his underwear, he stepped into the water so that he could support Montana against his body in the shower.

Even from across the room Misty could hear the sigh of relief from Montana as she rested back into Andy's arms.

'You OK, love?' Andy said.

'Now I am.' Montana looked across at Misty as the contraction eased away. 'Now's good for a listen.' And she smiled as Misty placed the Doppler again and Andy, too, could hear his baby.

When they'd listened to the heartbeat and were satisfied all was well, Misty stepped away. She turned off the bath and checked the temperature again before she and Ben withdrew outside the room.

'Now what?' Ben said as he glanced at the door Misty had closed behind her.

'Now we wait for fifteen minutes until I check baby again or until she wants to get into the bath. If they need me sooner, they'll ask.'

Misty had the equipment she needed in the bathroom and at that moment there was nothing to do except wait. She glanced at Ben and a smile tilted one side of his mouth as he caught her glance.

'I'll be good,' he teased softly, and she grinned.

There was something precious about sharing that moment outside the door with Ben, despite his obvious reservations, which she hadn't expected.

They smiled at each other and the connection she tried to tell herself didn't exist glowed between them until she looked away.

Ben leaned against the wall and studied her

face. 'So are you going to talk to me for the next fifteen minutes?'

She looked incredibly beautiful to him but still so painfully distant. He ached to reach out and touch her but, of course, he couldn't.

There were so many moments he'd thought they were getting there and then she'd back off again. The trouble was he couldn't stop feeling the way he did and he didn't believe she could either.

Whenever he tried to steer the conversation to them she redirected it to some other topic or left his presence. He needed to know if she too had memories she ached to relive like he did.

'I've talked to you every night on the veranda this week.' Misty's voice remained even and she picked up Montana's chart and began to fill it in.

He stayed at a distance and watched her. What was she thinking? He didn't get the way her mind worked. He wondered if he ever would.

'Of course you have. We talk about Tammy.' He ticked them off on his fingers. 'And Montana and Andy, and Ned and Louisa, and a lot about the unit. I want to talk about us.'

At that she glanced up and he felt his heart quicken as he waited for her response.

'Are you sure there is an "us", Ben?' she said. That wasn't quite what he'd hoped for.

'You need to spend time with your daughter,' she went on. 'Tammy needs you to focus on her.'

'I will. I intend to. But that doesn't mean I can't spend time with you, too.'

The reality was today he'd seen that maybe together he and Misty could do more for Tammy than he could by himself.

'I think together we could achieve great things. I couldn't have been wrong about the connection between us. I'd like to explore that further, or at least talk about it.'

She didn't look impressed with his tentative question but the words weren't coming easily. He didn't know for sure what he wanted. All he knew was that he wanted to spend a lot of his time near this woman.

'Explain what that means. What are you trying to say, Ben?'

He didn't know. It was hard to look into her cool green eyes as she dared him to be definite. The failures of the past rose up and haunted him.

Bridget, so unhappy she'd killed herself.

His patient that he'd failed so badly that she'd died.

His screwed-up daughter. He looked away. 'I don't know what I'm offering. More than just friends.'

He shrugged. 'Not marriage.' He bit his lip at the un-expected statement that had risen with such force. Well, at least she'd be able to tell he felt strongly about that.

She looked away so he couldn't read her expression and his flat declaration fell on the floor between them and lay there like spilt blood. He'd wounded her.

He hoped she'd understand and he tried to explain

but maybe he was making it worse. 'I'm not up for the wedding or happy family yet but to do everything else with you would be great.

'I've done marriage and it was a disaster. I don't think I'm husband material.'

She raised her chin. 'That's your baggage, Ben. Not mine. And it shouldn't have any bearing on anything between us.' She paused and looked back at him briefly. 'But I appreciate your honesty.'

Misty felt like clutching her heart because he'd just dashed any hope she'd had of this going any further. What had he expected her to say? She'd take what she could get?

Well, she wouldn't, because in the long run, if he carried too much emotional baggage to start fresh and positive with her and any children they might have together in the future, maybe being together wasn't the answer.

Misty glanced at her watch. Another five minutes before she could go into the bathroom. 'I can't talk about this now, Ben.'

But she could think about it. Add Tammy, who needed her father now more than ever, and there wouldn't be room for her in an equal relationship.

That wasn't too selfish, was it?

She'd waited all her life to feel the connection she felt with Ben and now she wasn't happy because she didn't have his undivided attention.

It was all so confusing and she wanted to be self-centred and hold out for the perfect relationship.

She knew people learnt to adapt to blended families, risked the difficulties for the joys of being with the person who made them feel whole, like Ben did to her, but was she one of those people?

These were questions she needed to answer for herself before she could talk to Ben about them. It was all too hard now.

What was he thinking to broach this subject now? The man's timing was way off!

Twelve minutes was close enough. She put the chart down and crossed the room to knock on the bathroom door.

'Good timing,' Andy said when she came in, because he'd just helped Montana into the bath. Montana paused so that Misty could listen to baby before she submerged her tummy.

After that, Andy climbed into the bath as well.

Misty glanced at Ben and his eyebrows had nearly disappeared into his hairline at husband and wife in the tub. He'd get used to it.

Montana rested her forearms on the edge of the tub while Andy rubbed her back. 'That is so wonderful,' she said.

She looked up at Misty. 'Pressure. It's getting close.'

Misty sat on the foam wedges they kept beside the bath and waited.

Ben couldn't believe how serene both women were. The only tension in the room came from him, and he tried to disappear into the walls and not invade their space.

Even Andy seemed focussed on his job of circular rubbing as his wife began to exhale slowly.

'OK. The head's coming through now,' Misty whispered, and Ben blinked in disbelief. There was no other sound from Montana or Misty and nobody made a move to deliver the baby.

He glanced at Andy, who had sat back and was watching as finally his wife put her arms down under the water to push the baby into her own hands.

Then it was over. They all stared at the baby with his wide blue eyes open under the water, and then Montana rotated his face down and lifted her son slowly to the surface.

When his face broke the surface he gasped and mewled and Montana floated him backward and forward so that Andy could see his legs and arms floating. Then she rested his downy cheek against her skin as she slid him along her body and up towards her breasts, where she nestled him and Andy wrapped his arms around them both.

Tears streamed down Andy's face and Ben admitted to some constriction in his own throat.

'We have our son. Jarrad,' Andy said gruffly, and Ben slipped from the room. They certainly didn't need him in there and he'd witnessed something he would never have believed he would be touched by.

But it was Misty's face that haunted him. She'd gazed with such raw sadness that his breath had jammed in his throat and he'd felt again the racking pain of his lungs on fire.

When she came out of the bathroom a few minutes later he was waiting. He held open his arms and to his huge relief she stepped into them.

Ben closed his eyes and rested his chin on her hair. Her scent shimmered around him and her body pressed firmly against his as he breathed. How could this not be right? He wanted this moment to last— just holding Misty.

This was why he'd come. He didn't know how much of himself he had to offer to her or if it was enough, but he knew his life could be vastly different with Misty in it and he wanted that. It would be more empty than ever without her there.

He'd rushed her and he vowed he wouldn't do that again. He would go slowly but he would win her and they would work something out. He had to believe that.

Misty sniffed and drew away. 'I'm so glad you were here to share Jarrad's birth. I'm an aunty. He's gorgeous.' She lifted her tear-stained face to his and he dropped a brief kiss on her lips because he couldn't not.

Misty stepped back and her next words returned him to earth with a bump. 'How do you think you'll be when it's Tammy's time?'

Oh, hell. He didn't even want to think about it, but he would have read everything he could get his hands on by then that might help. 'I guess I'll just have to have faith.'

Misty smiled at him through the tears still in her eyes. 'There's hope for you yet.'

'I'm glad to hear that.' And they both knew what he was saying.

An hour later Montana had settled into the ward bed for a rest and the phone rang at the desk.

'Is Ben there?' Louisa's voice on the phone held a thread of panic that Misty had never heard before.

'What's wrong, Louisa?'

'Tammy's gone.'

Misty glanced at the clock. It would be dark in an hour. 'Gone? Where?'

Misty's mind raced as she waited for Louisa's response. 'How do you know?' Where could she go on foot?

Louisa had more bad news. 'All her things are gone and I checked with the taxi service. They dropped her at the bus station after lunch. I rang there and they said Brisbane. She could be anywhere.'

Misty closed her eyes. Had she driven Tammy away? Had that touch of Ben's hand that Tammy had seen this morning been enough for her to feel *she* had betrayed her in some way?

Misty felt the crush of guilt and fear heavy in her chest. 'You did well to find out that much, Louisa. Ben's gone on a house call and won't be back for another hour.'

Ben would want answers. 'I'll leave a message when he comes back into range. Sara can come and finish my shift. I'll be home soon.'

When Misty arrived back at the residence Louisa held out the note. 'I just found this.'

The writing was messy, like Tammy's room, and brought home to Misty how young Ben's daughter really was. 'Tell Dad not to look for me,' the note said.

Ned and Louisa both looked grave. 'The wee one would'na talk to me at dinner.' Ned's accent had broadened with his concern and Misty hugged them both for their genuine distress about the young woman they had taken under their wing.

Misty sighed. 'Well, she talked to me this morning and I hope it wasn't anything I said. Ben will be here soon and he'll know where to look.'

She glanced at Louisa, who wrung her hands and looked tragically expectant, as if Misty could reassure her that Tammy would be fine. Ned looked miserable at Louisa's distress and Misty hugged them both again.

'We'll find her.' She looked at Louisa. 'Do you think you could make us a little hamper of food and a Thermos of coffee to take, please, Louisa?' Louisa needed distraction.

'And, Ned, can I borrow those maps of Queensland you were talking about the other night, please?'

The older couple nodded, relieved to have something to do, as Misty had intended, and she watched them go. How would Ben see this? He'd blame himself and fear the worst. She wished she knew what to do for the best.

For a brief second her sight shimmered and she saw Tammy's face surrounded by tears and shells, the shells of Ben's beach house.

Had Tammy gone to her father's house?

She'd never discussed her premonitions with Ben. How did she tell him that she'd had a vision when that was the last thing he would believe?

Louisa turned back as she reached the door. 'So you'll go with him?' she said.

Misty nodded. She didn't know how Ben would take it but she would. 'I'll ring Andy to cover while we're away and wait for Ben. Maybe you could mind Dawn if he gets called out?'

'Of course.' Louisa brightened considerably at the thought.

After the call, Misty tossed a few things into a small dufflebag and set it by the front door next to the little picnic hamper Louisa had brought.

Ben's face was white when he arrived and Misty silently handed him the note.

'I missed it again,' he said. 'I can't believe it. How could I do that?' He stared at the paper in his hand and Misty watched whatever had happened in the past rise and horrify him again.

'At least she called me Dad,' Ben said, but his

voice was grim. 'I'll make a few calls before I go. What about the hospital?'

'Andy will cover.' She caught his arm as he turned away. 'I'd like to come with you, Ben.'

This was a different man from the one at the beach or even on the ward. This was a cold, hard stranger who held her firmly out of his affairs. 'I don't think that would help Tammy.'

'For you, Ben.' Just today he'd said he wanted a future and they had to share the bad with the good, and this was a place to start. He had to let her share his worry. If there was any hope of them making it together, he needed to learn that he didn't have to be alone.

He wouldn't meet her eyes. 'Thank you, but I don't think so. I've made this mess, I've let down my daughter and all I can do is pray she hasn't done anything irrevocable.'

Haunted eyes met Misty's as she touched his hand. There was more here than she could guess if only he would let her in. All she knew was that she needed to be there for him, despite his efforts to shut her out.

Ben shook her off and turned away. 'You were the one who said I needed to spend more time with her. It looks like you were right. It's my fault she's gone and I need to find her. Perhaps not legally, but in here.' He thumped his chest. 'I'm her father.'

Misty watched him suffer and knew she couldn't let him go alone. She loved him. She admitted it now because all the pussyfooting around wasn't going to help Ben when he needed it most. She'd go if she had to tie herself to the front seat of his car, and if afterwards they went their separate ways then so be it. He needed her now.

'Today you said we should think about the future. Tammy will always be a part of your life. You are going to have to practise letting people into your life, Ben. You could start now with me.'

Ben sighed and he looked through Misty into the darkest part of his soul. 'What if I can't find her?'

'Then I'll be with you then, too.' Misty hesitated and then cast consequences to the wind. 'Sometimes I can find people when others can't. You have to trust me not to make matters worse, Ben.'

Ben frowned, unsure of what she meant, looked at her again as if he almost understood, then shrugged as if he didn't have the time to work it out. 'I'll pack and I'm leaving in five minutes.'

This was a new Ben she hadn't seen. Decisive, focussed as he should be when his daughter was missing, but coldly and clinically excluding her from his plans. She'd been afraid this could the reality of a relationship with Ben when things went wrong.

Misty sighed and straightened her shoulders. Now wasn't the time to bow out gracefully. She said goodbye to Louisa and Ned and carried her bags to Ben's car.

CHAPTER TEN

FIVE minutes later to the second Ben opened the driver's-side door and saw Misty waiting in the passenger seat.

He laughed once in that horrible mirthless humour she remembered from the beach. 'Determined little thing, aren't you?'

Misty refused to fight with him. 'Tammy is family. Did you find anything out from the phone calls?'

Ben started the car and revved it as if to release his frustration before he sighed and let the engine idle. 'Her grandmother says she hasn't seen her—who knows if that's true? But the housekeeper at the house will ring me if she turns up there. Tammy's switched her own mobile off but at least it's with her if she needs me.'

Thankfully the car took off smoothly as Ben regained his composure and Misty relaxed into the seat. 'So where are you going now?'

'Her mother's house.' His face looked grave. 'There's no one there but she knows where the key is.'

Misty couldn't rid her mind of the shells. 'I think you should go to the beach house.'

Ben frowned and turned to look at her. Unconsciously he slowed the car. 'Why? Did she say something?'

His voice hardened. 'When were you going to tell me?'

Misty's voice softened in comparison. 'If she'd said anything, I would have told you. But I think that's where she is.'

'There's a three-hour difference in direction.' Ben sighed and shook his head. 'If you know something I don't, explain.'

This was it. At least she wouldn't have to pretend it didn't exist. She'd never told anyone except two women friends and Andy. 'I have premonitions, Ben. Visions. That's how I found you the day you nearly drowned. I didn't see you fall into the water—I was looking for you.'

He glanced at her and his face closed. She'd known it would but she had to go on.

'I can see Tammy's face surrounded by shells. The ones in your bathroom at the beach house.'

There. She'd said it. He could make of it what he would. She couldn't help him any more.

Ben swore and Misty looked away from him out the window. Then he said, 'Great, another one,' ob-

scurely and glanced at his watch. She knew he was
thinking about how much time would be wasted if he
turned around and dropped her back at the residence.

Ben didn't say anything more and Misty leaned
back in the seat and closed her eyes. She felt sick!
The things you did for love.

It was a four-hour drive to the coast and Misty left
Ben to concentrate on the road as the shadows lengthened towards evening.

Once a bush wallaby skittered in front of the car
and Ben swerved suddenly, which threw Misty
forward against her seat belt. His hand came up as if
to protect her and connected with Misty's hand doing
the same thing. Their glances met.

He sighed and she glimpsed the Ben she knew
from a less stressful time. 'I'm sorry, Misty. I know
it's not your fault and you're trying to help. We'll talk
about the other thing later,' he said softly.

Comforted by his more even tone, the knot of
tension in Misty's neck eased. 'Actually, we've a
way to drive and, if you can, now could be a good
time to talk. There're things I want to know about
you, too, Ben.'

He stared straight ahead at the road in front. 'Like
what?' But he didn't say no and her shoulders relaxed
further in relief.

'Like why you brought Tammy to Lyrebird Lake.'

'Tammy at the lake has been a huge bonus.
Despite all her talk of me not being her father, we

have grown up with that relationship solid between us and that's come back a little in the short while we've been here. Despite Bridget's mother.'

Misty needed to clarify matters. 'Tammy's grandmother—the one she lived with?'

'Yes. That woman was one of the reasons her daughter was so screwed up. Bridget may have misled me into marriage but Tammy was the reason I stayed. I pray she's safe!'

She didn't understand and maybe they needed to go back further. 'So tell me about your marriage to Bridget.'

He sighed. 'There's nothing to tell. We grew up together, our fathers both ran their own companies and our mothers shared charities and boredom.'

He closed his eyes briefly. 'Bridget and I had been thrown together for years but we never planned to have a relationship.' He paused and glanced at Misty. 'She could hear voices.'

Misty drew in her breath.

Ben smiled crookedly and turned back to watch the road. 'Yeah. I should have realised then she was a disaster.'

Misty felt the world tilt as his words hit home. No wonder he'd said 'Great, another one,' when she'd said she knew where Tammy was. How ironic that her gift had brought Ben to her and now it was pushing him away.

Ben ploughed on as if once started he may as well

get it all over with. 'It seemed she needed a fall guy for another relationship that went wrong and she'd set the seduction up for that reason. Silly me.'

His breath whistled in the dark. 'But she did need me to be stable for her. She was drowning in well-camouflaged mental illness even then. I looked after her, submerged myself in my work when I needed sanity myself, and stayed in our marriage for Tammy. But I couldn't make Bridget happy. I honestly don't think anyone could. When she died her mother made them call it unresolved postnatal depression, which dumped the guilt back onto me, as an obstetrician who should have seen that coming, along with the bombshell of Tammy's paternity.'

His voice lowered. 'Then something at work happened and I lost the plot.'

The inflection on 'something' told Misty this was the real reason Ben was afraid. She let the silence build. Already he'd shared more than she'd expected, and she could wait if he wanted to stop now.

The miles passed and Misty closed her eyes until she heard Ben shift in his seat.

Misty straightened. 'Let's stop for coffee. Louisa has made a hamper. Five minutes to stretch your legs.'

'You're a mind-reader.' He looked at her and smiled at the unintentional pun. 'Do you do that, too?'

Misty smiled back and the weight of his scepticism eased. Another fragment of their rapport returned and Misty was very glad she'd come.

Ten minutes later they were back on the road. They'd had a normal conversation at the truck stop and now they were both wide awake.

'Do you still want to know about my patient?'

Misty tried not to let him hear her sigh of relief. 'What happened, Ben?'

She heard him breathe deeply once in the dark and then he began. 'One of those tragedies we all dread. It should have been simple. Twin pregnancy. She'd had twins before, everything looked fine—ultrasounds perfect, then something went wrong, we never found out what. And one of the twins died unexpectedly. I did an emergency Caesarean and we saved the second twin but the family, of course, were devastated.'

He stopped again and when he resumed his voice was even softer, as if he was afraid to tell the story out loud. 'I kept thinking what I could have done differently. Should I have had them more closely watched, done more blood tests, induced them earlier? I felt so useless and that I'd let them down. I started to dread that if something like that happened again, would I act differently?' There was no doubt what she was hearing had affected him profoundly.

'When my patient returned for her postnatal visit I was distracted. I shouldn't have been distracted at work. Bridget had died and I was in mid-disaster with Tammy's custody, but that's no excuse.'

It might not be an excuse but it explained a lot, Misty thought, but she didn't interrupt his flow.

He sighed. 'I knew something wasn't right. She looked the same, her second twin was immaculate and growing well, and she said she was fine. The baby was sleeping but she seemed brittle. Almost frozen into a caricature of herself. I persevered a little on her mental state but she was adamant she was happy.'

He slapped the steering-wheel. 'I should have done more, never have let her go.' He sighed again. 'I suspected she was depressed and gave her emergency numbers to call, even arranged a visit with a psychiatrist the next day, which she wasn't keen on. And then I rang her husband.'

Misty cleared her throat and swallowed. 'So you think she had postnatal depression or postnatal psychosis?'

Ben nodded. 'That afternoon she leapt from her apartment window with her baby in her arms. They both died.'

Misty felt the cold of shock douse her skin. 'That's horrible.'

'So was the court case,' he said wryly, as he switched on the indicator and turned onto another road. She wondered how he could still concentrate on driving. She looked at his face as the sudden light from a streetlamp illuminated it, and it was as if he was carved from stone.

The streetlight passed and his voice came out of

the darkness. 'I admitted I suspected something and didn't do enough, and the family wanted to sue me for the shirt off my back.' He gave that mirthless laugh she decided she hated.

'As if I'd care about that. They could have it all. I did care, very much, that I'd failed her. And her baby. I hadn't been able to save either of her children and now she had died in my care as well.'

He turned to Misty and rubbed his palm on his leg, as if to wipe away the despair. A truck approached and passed and in the moment of light she could see the pain in his furrowed brow, as if it was all still beyond his comprehension that it could have happened.

Misty laid her hand over his and squeezed his fingers in comfort. He looked surprised at first and then, as if unable to stop himself, he squeezed Misty's hand in gratitude.

He flicked a glance at her as if she too should condemn him. 'She'd previously been a normal mother. Postnatal depression affected her brain after the birth, which didn't allow her to cope with grief. I let her down. I've had to live with that. It's been hard.'

Even through his fingers Misty could feel the waves of despair, even after all this time, and she wondered out loud. 'How long ago did this happen?'

He took his hand out from under hers and put it back on the wheel, as if he'd had all the sympathy he deserved. 'Three years last November.' The lack of expression in his voice was sadder than anything.

'Who was there for you, Ben?' This had happened after the devestation of Bridget taking her own life and the custody battle for Tammy. It was a miracle he was sane.

She wanted to tell him to pull over so she could hug him and tell him he'd done his best. Somebody should have. 'And you left obstetrics after that?'

'I had no heart for it. And I didn't fancy letting anyone else down.'

'And your friends and colleagues?' Misty didn't understand. Didn't men talk to other men like women talked to each other? Like the midwives supported each other over sad events and the fickleness of nature? Obviously not. 'Your family? Have you talked to anyone else about this?'

'Sure,' he said, and she didn't like the undercurrent in that one word. 'I talked to my lawyer, the judge and the court.'

Not quite therapeutic. 'And?'

His tone was flat, like the judgment. 'The QC said perhaps I could have done more but it had been an unfortunate series of events out of my control. It was suggested I could do further studies in the psychiatry of obstetrics and document the findings. I left clinical obstetrics and did just that.'

Leaving a gaping hole where he should have completed the process of grief, Misty thought. He should have gone back to see the joyful side of birth again.

Ben went on. 'I settled half of my bank account on the family, despite the court ruling in my favour.'

He laughed mirthlessly yet again and Misty winced. 'The amusing part is that I've made another fortune with the reference book I wrote on the subject, but at least it might help identify other women at risk out there.

'All future royalties are shared between Tammy…' He hesitated as his daughter's disappearance caught up with him, then completed the sentence. 'And donated to Beyond Blue, an organisation dedicated to supporting sufferers of depression.'

He looked across at her. 'That was all I could do.'

Now Misty understood why Ben feared depression with Tammy's pregnancy. Because not only would he lose Tammy, he wouldn't be able to survive if any thing happened.

'When my patient died, I realised I'd failed another person. Bridget's mother took Tammy because she hated me for not being able to save her daughter. I still don't know what I could have done differently.'

He shook his head as if to rid himself of the thought. 'It doesn't matter. So I did what I could for Tammy from a distance. I grew to like my isolated life. My only visitors were Tammy for occasional weekends and my editor.'

Ah, Ben. She undid her seat belt and leaned across to kiss his cheek. Because she had to. 'You were hiding, but you can't hide any more because Tammy needs you.'

He looked at her as she buckled herself in again. 'And you.' He looked back at the road and then flicked another glance at Misty. 'You're the mermaid who dragged me from the ocean and made me join the world again.'

He paused and then said, 'Now I have to believe your "vision" that tells you Tammy is safe and at the beach house. Do you realise how hard that is for me? I escaped into the science of mental illness to distance myself from the things I didn't trust or identify with, and now because of you I have to go there again.'

Now she understood a little more. Why he fought against the concept of the birth centre where instinct and faith in the natural mechanisms of the human body were the most important things.

In context he'd done very well to be as calm as he had. And now he drove to the place she'd said his daughter would be. Not because of something he believed in but because he believed in *her*.

Tammy was at the beach house. Red-eyed from crying and huddled in the big squishy armchair with her arms wrapped around herself. 'I don't want to come back with you,' she said.

Ben looked at Misty and then back at his daughter and sighed. 'You can't have your baby by yourself. You need to have people who care about you for support.'

'You don't mean that. You're just saying that. I know you don't need me in your life now you've found Misty.' She turned away and Misty had no doubt it was to hide her tears. Ben was getting nowhere and she could tell he was hurting.

Misty looked at him and signalled with her eyes to give her a chance. Tammy was so young and any parent knew there were problems when an extra person appeared in family dynamics. Maybe Tammy would listen to her or at least tell her what she thought of her.

Tammy frowned as she watched her father leave and she untangled herself from the chair as if she was going to follow him. Then she turned back to Misty.

Her shoulders were hunched as she stood there with her arms folded on top of her big belly and glared at the interloper, or that was what Misty felt herself.

Misty wasn't sure where to start. 'Your father is trying. He wants to be there for you and your baby.'

'I don't need him.' Tammy sniffed. 'I don't need anybody.'

'Do you know who you sound like? Your father.' Misty felt like smiling but was sure Tammy would take it the wrong way if she did. 'Everybody needs somebody. That's what I'm trying to tell your father. There can never be too many people in your life. Come back to Lyrebird Lake. You have friends and family there.'

Tammy turned away. 'I don't have friends.'

'You have Emma and Louisa,' Misty said quietly. 'I thought Emma was going to come in with you when you have your baby. And Louisa and Ned are worried about you, and that's not good for them at their age.'

Tammy sniffed. 'I am sorry about that because they're all nice, but I'm not coming back.'

Misty moved to stand beside her. 'Things happen in life that we want to run away from, but that's not always the answer.'

Misty met Tammy's eyes. 'Yes, your father and I have found we might have something together, and I'm not sure if that's going to go somewhere yet or not, but what happens with us isn't a good reason for you to lose out.

'Do you really want to throw your chance away to share the early months of your baby with your family and friends? That's a gift some people don't have. It will be during one of the most important times in your life. The other options short-change you and your baby.'

Tammy turned her face away. 'I'd rather miss that than be in the way.'

Misty wanted to hug her but she was scared Tammy would push her away. 'Oh, Tammy. You won't be in the way. How could you? You drew Ben and I together when we would never have seen each other again. Thanks to you, I did get a chance to get to know someone who makes me feel as no one else has ever done. Your dad is an amazing man. And he loves you very much. I'd hate to be the cause of a separation between two people who have as special a bond as you and your dad.'

Tammy still fought being swayed but Misty could sense the change because even Tammy knew her arguments were thin.

When Tammy didn't speak Misty went on. 'What if you go into labour somewhere you don't know anybody? You'll be on your own except for the midwife. Not all hospitals are as peaceful as at the lake. You need to remember family is much more important than pride.'

'You're not my family,' Tammy said softly.

'Oh, Tammy.' Misty put her hand on Tammy's arm and squeezed it gently. 'I'd like to be.'

Tammy looked at her stone-faced. 'My father won't marry you.'

Misty's face remained serene. 'What makes you think he needs to?'

Tammy rolled her eyes. 'Anyone can see you two are besotted with each other.'

'I hope not,' Misty said, 'because we're not there yet. I don't think your father needs another relationship right now.'

Tammy's eyes narrowed. 'My mother killed herself when she was married to him.'

Misty's voice softened. 'And you think that's Ben's fault?'

'That's what my grandmother says.' Tammy didn't meet Misty's eyes.

Misty forgot about the horrible trip, the pain Tammy had caused her father and the selfishness of her youth, and just felt like hugging her. Poor kid. Misty tried to imagine losing her mother, then being told the other parent she loved was a monster.

There were some sad people in the world and Tammy's grandmother must be the saddest. 'I understand that's what your grandmother says—but what do you say, Tammy?' she asked quietly.

To Misty's relief Tammy shrugged her shoulders at the ridiculousness of the concept. 'You're kidding me. Of course it's not Dad's fault.'

Misty released the breath she hadn't realised she'd been holding. Even if Tammy didn't believe it, there would be fallout from such a negative upbringing. Why had Ben left her with that woman? 'Do you think your father should spend his whole life being sorry that he couldn't save your mother?'

Tammy stood up and kicked a shoe across the room. 'Yes.'

Misty raised her eyebrows. 'Well, that was honest, at least. But doesn't he deserve to be happy?'

Tammy didn't say anything.

Misty took a step closer and her voice was quiet. 'You're not with your grandmother now, Tammy. You're old enough to have a baby and you're old enough to make your own decision about your father's culpability. You have to decide what you're going to tell your child. Think about what you really believe.'

Tears formed in Tammy's eyes and trickled down her cheeks. 'But if he didn't make her kill herself then it's my fault. Mum had postnatal depression after having me and it never went away.'

Misty stood up and went to the door. 'Ben, come in here, please.'

She risked tugging Tammy gently into her arms for a quick hug, and to her relief Tammy didn't push her away. 'Please, tell your father that because he needs to know that's how you feel.'

Ben appeared at the door and Misty let go of Tammy and gestured him in.

'Tammy,' she prompted, and looked encouragingly at Ben's daughter to share her fear with Ben.

'Mum had postnatal depression after having me and it never went away. It's my fault she died.'

Ben crossed the room and swept his daughter into his arms. 'That's not true, Tammy,' he said. 'Oh, baby. Your mother had an illness before she had you. She had depression and, like some illnesses do, it killed her. It's not your fault and, you know, it's not mine either. And—' his voice firmed '—it's not going to happen to you. I love you and worry about you a lot, and deep inside I know you would never do that.'

Suddenly Tammy burrowed her face in Ben's neck and hugged him. 'I do want to come back and it was so horrible at the bus station all by myself. Are you very cross with me?'

'No, baby. I love you,' Ben said.

Misty smiled at the both of them. 'Your father hates it when the people he loves are hurting. You should have seen him when he was coming to look for you. A wild bull couldn't have stopped him.'

Tammy smiled through her tears. 'He's a pretty cool dad, you know.' She sniffed and wiped her eyes. 'I'll come back.'

'I'm glad,' Misty said, and she had to tilt her head to see into Tammy's face. 'How come you got to be so beautiful and tall?'

'My dad's really tall,' she said as she looked at Ben, and they all laughed.

Ben held out his arm and Misty joined the group hug then she pulled back. 'I'll leave you two alone while I ring Louisa and Ned and tell them the good news.'

'Thank you. Misty.' Ben squeezed her hand which he seemed to have been holding for hours.

'Again,' he mocked himself. 'You seem to be making a habit of saving me. You realise you can't ever leave me or I'll backslide into the morose person I was before I met you.'

They stood on the veranda of the beach house and the moon was rising out of the waves in the distant ocean.

Misty looked at this man who had come into her

life with such impact. Gorgeously imperfect but he knew he had faults and she'd begun to think he just needed to learn she loved him unconditionally. She'd just realised that herself.

'You don't have to do everything by yourself, Ben. If we're going to be a part of each other's lives you need to learn to let me into all of it, not just the easy bits.'

He pulled her against him and settled his arm around her shoulder. 'I've never been the type of guy to tell people what's happening inside me. I'd always believed men needed to be strong and in control. You don't play by those rules. You still think we have a chance?'

She looked up at him and rested the point of her finger on his chest and poked him gently. 'If you try.'

He laughed. 'Ow. I'm trying.'

Misty resisted the impulse to poke him again but he knew she wanted to. 'Then try harder.'

He dropped a kiss on her lips and then another, as if he couldn't settle for just that one, then he put her away from him. 'Come for a walk on the beach. I'd like to show you my special haunts.'

She recognised that buzz that ran up her arm and down into her belly. 'Are you planning to try and seduce me?'

'That, too,' he said, and his eyes met hers with wicked warmth that left no doubt of his meaning.

'What about Tammy?' Misty glanced into the house.

'Tammy's fine. Tucked up in bed and sleeping the dreams of the innocent. Thanks to you. She's exhausted and told me she's glad we came to find her. She said she really does want to have her baby at the lake. And that she likes you.'

He looked across at the moonlit beach in the distance. 'Come and see. We won't be back here while I'm at the lake.'

Misty listened to the sounds of the ocean and nodded. Of course he missed it here. 'You should drive over on your days off.'

He raised his eyebrows suggestively. 'Will you come with me?'

'If I can. Or you and Tammy could come.' She had commitments, too, and they'd need to work things out.

They walked through low silver dunes that rolled between the house and the beach and the sand was still warm from the day's heat even though it was dark.

The crashing of the waves grew louder and when they topped the last rise the moon shone a path through the swells and breaking waves out to the horizon.

Misty breathed in the tang of salt and dug her toes in the sand. 'It looks as though we could walk across the water to the moon it's so bright.'

Ben was looking at only her. 'You make me feel that way all the time I'm with you.'

He stopped in a warm bowl of sand on top of the last sand dune and they looked out over the waves. On the headland the lighthouse blinked its beam out to sea towards the place where they'd met.

Misty tilted her cheek into the breeze and breathed deeply again with her eyes shut. 'Glorious,' she whispered, and she could feel the wind lift her hair and the pricking of granules of sand as they swirled around her ankles.

There was something primal about that night, with the ocean and the sky fused in silver.

When Ben rested his fingers gently on both her cheeks she opened her eyes.

He smiled at her. 'I wanted to capture the moonlight on your face. You awe me. Your strength, your compassion for my daughter and myself. I'm so fortunate to have met you.'

'Destiny, do you think?'

'At the very least,' he said, and drew her towards him until their lips met and there was intent in his caress.

She should have said no but this was Ben.

She lifted her hand and rested her fingers in his and followed his lead.

He cradled her face like a precious bowl and she saw there in his eyes the quiet hope that made her wish to be as daring as he was, as positive as he was that all would turn out well.

'Tell me, Ben,' she whispered, 'why do you have the power to fascinate me?' She could no more deny him than the breath of life.

'Because...' he said on a smile, and when he kissed her this time it was a journey home to a place they both belonged and he made the tears spring to her eyes just with the joy of being there with him, that connection from the first touch.

'I love you,' he finished against her mouth.

There it was again. The perfect union of breath and nuance that captured her heart and squeezed it just as Ben's arms had captured and enfolded her into the magical space that could even exclude the glories of nature around them.

When he eased her down into the hollow of sand she lay back and watched as he knelt above her and drew off his shirt. The moon silvered the expanse of his chest in planes of dark and light and his arms corded as he lifted her head and slipped the fabric, still warm from his body, under her hair to soften the sand.

His fingers trailed along her cheek and she turned her face into his palm and kissed him. 'I hope your daughter can't look out of a window and see us.'

'We can't see the house from this knoll and the house can't see us,' he murmured as he undid the buttons on her shirt. He sighed as her top spread open before him to reveal her lace-covered breasts.

He said something she didn't expect. 'I've never made love in the moonlight before. Will you share this first with me?'

She reached up and brushed his lips with her fingers and she hoped the answer was in her eyes.

There was no doubt he understood. 'I want to worship you tonight.'

The sand was warm when the backs of her hands

uncurled with the sensations. Ben's fingers stroked each layer of clothing away and saluted each section of bared skin. His eyes were hot and intent on undressing her until she was exposed to the moon on a pile of discarded clothes he kept layering under her.

Misty felt strangely exultant to be naked to the breeze in the moonlight. She felt powerful, cherished and earthy with Ben right there beside her.

Where she lay was protected from the breeze by the rim of the saucer, with the stars blazing above and the sound of the ocean just over the hill. 'It's like a secret world up here. So beautiful.'

'It certainly is,' he whispered, and knelt half-turned above her to run his hand from the hollow of her throat, between her breast and over her stomach. He paused, soaking heat into her stomach as his palm rested over it, then he bent and kissed the sensitive skin of her belly and she trembled with anticipation as his skin slid along hers so he lay on his side and gazed at her.

They should talk about the future. 'Ben, we should talk…'

'Later…' he whispered. Then he kissed her and there was no more time for talk. His thigh covered hers as his mouth slid from her lips to plunder lower, and then back up again as he worshipped her. The sweetness of tasting him, his flavour meshed with their heat, the feel of her softness moulded against his corded strength and the possessive trail of his reverent fingers over her hip. When she touched him it felt as though she had the same power in her own hands.

She should have felt as awkward, clumsy as an inexperienced lover, but this was Ben. At this moment she could seduce and entice and please her lover with every nuance of movement she made.

Misty arched away from the cushioning sand into him and the sensations swept away all thought of anywhere but here with Ben.

They rose together on a wave that didn't touch the sand and Ben's whisper drifted again into the night sky. 'I love you, Misty.'

Afterwards they wandered hand in hand down to the ocean, kissing as they went, and once there they splashed naked in the shallows like children. The water slid across her skin like velvet and everything was perfect except for the tiny unease that Ben didn't want to talk about the future.

CHAPTER ELEVEN

THREE weeks later Misty looked across the kitchen at Tammy and Ben laughing at some private joke that amused them and she smiled. Things were going well.

They had agreed to concentrate on Tammy until after her baby was born before they explored their own relationship. Secretly Misty was glad because, despite their physical closeness, something she couldn't doubt, she still harboured fears that Ben could never share the rest of his life with anyone until he'd exorcised his demons.

Misty stifled a yawn as she glanced at the clock. She only had an hour till she needed to get to work but she was having trouble motivating herself this morning.

Nagging nausea made her look at her toast with a sudden tide of revulsion and she stood up, almost knocking her chair over in her haste to get to the bathroom in time.

She could feel Ben's eyes on her back as she left the room but she didn't have time to stop.

'Here, let me help,' Ben said quietly as he followed her into the bathroom and lifted her ponytail away from her face. 'I seem to remember doing this for you before.'

His hand came down and cupped her forehead. She dabbed her mouth with the cloth that suddenly appeared. 'Obviously you make me throw up,' she said in a poor attempt at humour.

'I remember how I did that last time but would you like to enlighten me on what I did on this occasion?'

'You know as much as I do. Excuse me.' She stood up and glanced with meaning towards the door before she crossed to the sink to clean her teeth.

'We'll talk about this tonight,' Ben said, as if he knew she needed time to think things through on her own first.

Later that morning Misty had trouble concentrating and it was not a good time for that to happen.

The hospital seemed crazily busy, not just in the birth centre but Casualty and the wards, and Misty missed Montana's help so much that Andy had promised to fly down at the weekend and pick up Mia, a friend and fellow midwife, in his plane.

The up side so far, she decided, was that Ben had no time to drop into the birth centre while she struggled with the suspicion that had settled in her brain.

Was she pregnant with Ben's child?

At morning tea she slipped unnoticed into the storeroom in Casualty and found the box containing the pregnancy kits. She chewed her lip as she stared at it.

When she left, she felt the package absurdly heavy against her hip, as if she had a time bomb in her pocket, and she tried not to think about the ramifications if she used it.

Throughout the rest of the day she tried to clear her head a little before the intended 'discussion' that evening.

Ben waited outside her room after she'd changed from her workclothes so that when she came out she couldn't avoid him before the evening meal.

'We need to talk. Come for a walk with me, Misty,' he said. 'Outside the house away from interruptions.' The look in his eyes struck a chord deep inside her chest.

She sighed. Yes. They did need to do this. Maybe she was even ready.

She nodded and he took her hand as if this was a ritual every evening, and suddenly it didn't seem to be the time to fight that assumption.

They crossed the road from the house and he drew her to the path that meandered along the lakefront under the trees.

It was cooler as the sun moved towards the west and a slight breeze lifted the ends of her hair and blew them across her face.

'I think we need to establish a few things,' Ben

began, and Misty heaved a sigh of relief. She'd never had cause to think Ben would lie and the opportunity to be honest seemed long overdue.

'Good,' she said, and turned her head to look at him as he tightened his fingers on hers.

'Shall we sit?' he suggested, and drew her to one of the park benches that lined the path. When they sat his hip nudged warmly against hers and it felt good just touching him.

She glanced around and they were alone for the moment. She wondered if she could whisper the words that loomed so large in her mind.

'It's seven weeks since I met you,' Ben said.

Misty drew a deep breath and the words tumbled out. 'It's three weeks since we made love.'

His finger came across and lifted her chin so that he could see her face. 'Yes, it is. Three crazily busy weeks since I first said I love you. Why...' he looked at her searchingly '...have you begun to doubt that?'

'I'm not sure.'

His eyes softened. 'Does this morning have something to do with this indecision?'

'Yes!' She looked away, at anything else but his face, and then she looked back at him again. 'I'm sure you can guess. I might be pregnant! And I don't know what I think about that, let alone what you will think about it.'

Ben stilled and his hand froze as if even though he'd suspected it, he was shocked to hear her say it out loud.

When he didn't take her hand or say anything she continued, 'I've never been late before and my breasts are tender.'

Ben sat back and closed his eyes. When he opened them he smiled ruefully at Misty, and she saw he was connecting her behaviour towards him with this news.

He nodded. 'Thus your edginess with me. It makes sense.' He frowned. 'It may have been a sand dune but I took precautions.' He grinned ruefully. 'Lots of them.'

She rolled her eyes. 'One of them didn't work.'

Quietly his voice broke the afternoon stillness. 'Obviously. How long have you known?'

'I don't "know" officially yet. Without expecting miracles, I wondered if you'd like to be with me when I do the test?'

His whole face softened and she felt the tears prick her eyes as she saw how much this small thing meant to him. How easily she could have excluded him and missed that.

'Thank you.' He looked away and then back again, and she wondered what emotion he hadn't wanted her to see. 'I appreciate the chance of inclusion,' he said.

The chance. Misty heard his words and her stomach dropped. Was he considering declining his participation?

Finally Ben lifted her hand and dropped a kiss in

her palm. 'This will take some getting used to. Imagine if we had a daughter and I'd have to go through all this pregnancy stuff again,' he shuddered. 'I don't know if I'm ready for this.'

'Not a lot of choice here, Ben. And if it makes you feel any better, neither am I. But nobody is going to force you to stay.'

He looked at Misty and smiled. 'There's no chance of me leaving. Just give me a minute. You're a bit ahead of me with the idea.'

'Maybe there's nothing to worry about.' She said it but deep inside she knew the truth. But it would give her more time before something was said that maybe she didn't want to hear.

Ben stood up and she wasn't sure how to construe his eagerness to put the matter beyond doubt. 'Let's go find out, then.'

Half an hour later they stood together in the bathroom at the residence with the door shut.

The second pink line couldn't be denied and Misty sagged against the wall. She'd known. Now Ben did and she couldn't escape the consequences.

'Come on,' Ben said. 'No one knows we're here. Let's go back to the lake and talk about this.'

They escaped out the side door of the house like truant children. The sun had set but it was still light enough to see.

Once they reached the path again it was darker and

quiet, with no other walkers, and every now and then the splash of a fish jumping in the water could be heard in the distance.

They'd walked a fair way before Ben broke the silence. 'You OK?' he asked.

'Yes.' I'm scared, she thought. 'I think so.'

Ben drew her to their bench but once there and seated, he didn't say anything.

Misty sat with her hands folded and tried not to read anything negative into his silence as she gazed out over the lake.

He'd never offered marriage, had already stated he didn't want to do happy families, and now they both knew she was pregnant. What would she really settle for?

He took her hand that had lain bereft in her lap as he decided their fate. She could feel herself begin to bristle. He'd taken his time. It wasn't hard. In or out!

'I'm sorry, Misty. For not having the instant answer when there can only be one answer.'

Misty tried not to hope too much.

He went on. 'Believe me, I've come a long way, because a month ago I wouldn't have considered any kind of relationship, let alone a long-term one. But I haven't been able to get you out of my head. I fell in love with you, Misty, long before we lay beneath the stars on the beach and made our baby.'

She heard him but she'd heard nothing that really

filled her with certainty. 'I'm worried, Ben. You don't really know me or I you.'

This time his voice held no indecision. 'I know what's important.' He squeezed her hand and looked deep into her eyes. 'You are important. To me. The rest we'll find out as we go through life together. If you'll have me.'

She went to speak but he held up his hand. 'Before you say anything, let me explain my hesitation before you construe it as reluctance. I'm not reluctant, Misty. Far from it.'

He squeezed her hand again and looked earnestly into her face. 'This is my problem. How am I going to ask you to marry me without you thinking it's only because we might have a baby?'

'It is a problem,' she said dryly.

He shook his head. 'But it's not true. Apart from the fact we spontaneously combust when we touch, I know there is a strong basis between us to work from. Surely you can see that I care for you too much to let you go, even if you weren't pregnant.'

Strong basis? They were discussing a baby, not foundations for a house. No doubt he meant the sex. 'So you're saying because the sex is good we can hope to share the parenting of our child.'

He slid his hand around the back of her neck and pulled her close to kiss her eyelids and then each side of her mouth. When their lips finally met Misty felt the vibration down to her toes.

'The kissing is pretty awesome, too,' he said, and Misty blinked as Ben sat back with a small, tender smile on his face.

Ben went on, 'And, of course, we'll share the parenting!'

'Why's that, Ben?'

He smiled that blinding, one-hundred-watt smile he only brought out on the rarest occasions and she blinked even in the dim light. 'I love you so much I can't imagine going back into the dark without you.'

He shrugged ruefully. 'I would have liked to have you to myself for a while, but we've still got nine months.'

She could feel excitement building. It would be OK. Maybe it wouldn't be so hard. He'd taken this on board much better than she'd dare to hope.

Ben squeezed her hands between his. 'What about the part where I get to hold you in my arms and wake up beside you?'

Misty could feel herself being pulled in closer, and not just physically. 'I didn't know I'd offered that.' The reaction was happening again and this was why she'd had to keep her distance. She had no defences against him.

He leaned towards her and there was nothing she could do to stop him because she'd been thinking about kissing him for three weeks.

When his lips touched hers it was like the beach house all over again. Why? How could he have such power? she thought fleetingly as her brain swirled away to focus on the touch and taste of his mouth against hers.

His arms came up and she was cradled against him where she'd wanted to be since she'd been with him in the sand. He pulled back for a moment so that he could see her face, and the tenderness she saw there made tears well in her eyes.

'You know that thing I said about not being a marrying man?'

'Yes…'

'It's not true. I wouldn't be able to live the happy and fulfilled life I can now see in front of me if I wasn't married to you.' He stopped and turned her to him so she could see the sincerity and love in his face. 'Please, marry me, Misty Buchanan.'

'Are you sure, Ben?'

'If you didn't love me, there's no way you'd put up with me.'

'True.'

'So marry me. I love you more each day and I didn't think that was possible.'

'And I love you, too, but you'd better improve with age.'

He looked around at the dying light and the last of the reflection shining off the lake and back at her in his arms. 'At this moment my life is perfect. You know, the day you left me all those weeks ago, I couldn't get you out of my mind.'

He went on. 'You need to know that my need to see you dragged me out of my safe bubble. Do you know how hard that was? Because of you, I had to uproot myself from the beach, follow you here, and even go back to working in a hospital, which I said I'd never do again.'

'And Tammy.'

'My darling daughter is my excuse, not the reason I'm here. We could have got to know each other somewhere else but it would never have been as nurturing as you have made it here. Jut another facet of how much I owe you.'

He kissed her. 'All the angst and change and facing the past has been so worth it because of what I've found with you.'

He kissed her again. 'Because finally I have you in my arms and I'm not letting you go.'

'So you think we could stay here for a while?'

'Because you're here I could stay anywhere. But I love the lake and the healing it's brought. I'm sorry I was sceptical when I got here. I was pretty bad, wasn't I?'

'You were very sceptical,' Misty agreed.

He grinned. 'Do you forgive me?'

'I admit you were under stress.' She tilted her head at him, considering. 'I'll think about suitable compensation.'

His eyes darkened and she felt the clench in her gut he could cause just by inference. She was a basket case.

'I like the sound of that,' he said.

Not that kind of compensation, but she couldn't help the secret smile that curved her lips. 'You may not like my idea. I think I'll get you to do a talk at the young mums' class on complications in pregnancy. And share the babysitting I have to do for Montana and Andy's anniversary at the end of this week.'

'I think I could handle both of those if you were there.'

The promise of other compensations shimmered between them and she tried to distract herself from inviting him to do more than just kiss her here in the dark. Now that she'd discovered how it felt to be with Ben she didn't know how she was going to last until she could be with him again. She hoped he was good at organizing fast weddings. The man was turning her into a nymphomaniac.

Misty hid her smile as an amusing thought crossed her mind. 'You known I have this vision of you surrounded by crying babies. Maybe I'm having triplets. Three daughters.'

He couldn't hide his horror. 'You saw this? You're kidding!'

She laughed. 'Yes. I'm kidding. No vision.'

He wiped his brow with mock relief then looked down at her indiscernible pregnancy. 'I wonder if our child will be able to save the person they love, like you saved me?'

'Will you mind too much if they do?'

'How could I? Without your gift I wouldn't be here. But promise me you'll never leave me, especially surrounded by crying babies.'

She rested her head on his shoulder, finally able to believe that everything would turn out right. Ben did love her and they would make a wonderful life together. 'I'll never leave you, my love, and as for the babies, we'll see.'

'As long as we're together,' he said, and the wonder in his voice made tears spring to her eyes.

'Despite the fact that you can be hard work, I love your company, your crazy-man ways and the way you make me feel like I'm the most special person in the world.'

He looked down at her. 'You've taken *me* on— you'd have to be the most special person in the world.'

He grinned at a thought. 'You know I'm going to be just as horrible to your midwife when you go into labour. I'll be even more of a mess.'

'Impossible,' she said, and laughed up at him. He caught her hand and pulled her to him.

'I'm pretty basic. I can't stand seeing the women I love in pain.'

'Ah, but what a cause.'

They didn't wait. The wedding was held the next week, on the beach at midday, because Ben said that's where his new life had begun, thanks to Misty.

The bride wore champagne silk and the groom's tie

matched her gown as it kissed her ankles and floated above her bare feet as she crossed the fine sand.

The trouser legs of Ben's suit were rolled up at the bottom as he stood and waited for her to join him on the shore.

Misty saw the waves breaking ahead of her as she walked towards him. The man who had changed so much in her life and made her realise the strength and vulnerability that came from loving another person with such depth.

Ben looked so strong and tall yet with such love shining from his face as he watched her approach that she blinked tears away because today was for joy.

Ben was her man, her soulmate, and there would be trials and laughter, and a world of love with him because she would be an equal partner in their journey to celebrate life.

Later, on top of the cliff, the guests milled joyfully outside the tall white lighthouse that looked over the ocean and the windows were open in the sprawling keeper's cottage to let the scent of the ocean blow through the revellers as they partied.

When the guests had departed, Misty and Ben strolled along beside the white picket fence that marched crisply around the cliff edge and over-looked the ocean below. Ben held firmly to his wife's hand as they gazed over the ocean that had brought them together.

He lifted Misty's hand to his lips and dropped a

gentle kiss on the inside of her wrist. 'To my wife, my life, my love,' he said, and pulled her back against him so he could rest his hands protectively over her stomach.

'Thank you for saving me and now I'm going to save you for the rest of your life.'

CHAPTER TWELVE

TAMMY LOOKED BACK AT the waiting room where she'd spent the morning in early labour. 'Can Emma come?'

Louisa spoke up. 'I can mind Grace, if Emma will let me. I'd love to.'

'Emma?' Misty smiled at the girl. She knew Emma would love to be with Tammy the whole way through.

Emma looked at Tammy. 'If you think it would help you, of course I'll come.'

Which meant Ben was superfluous and was left standing outside the bathroom door, as he'd known he would be.

Ben looked at Misty as she passed in front of him after his daughter. 'What if she needs me?'

Misty paused. 'As soon as she asks we'll call you in. You'll have to wait for that, Ben.'

He stood forlornly outside the bathroom door and listened to his daughter moan. He became more and more distressed. He paced, he tried to read, he walked to the residence and back, and finally he sat outside the door with his head in his hands and tried not to listen.

Inside the room Misty could see that Tammy was fine between contractions, even laughed occasionally, and moaned because that was the noise her body told her to make.

'Good opening noises,' she said to Tammy, and Emma encouraged her to let the sound out.

By late afternoon Tammy's time was close.

Misty went to see how Ben was faring and, not at all to her surprise, he looked a mess. She put her arms around him and hugged him.

'What are you doing to her in there?' Ben shook his head as he tried to speak rationally despite all the fear that bubbled inside him.

Misty stepped back and gazed at the man she loved, thought about how hard it must be to be only hearing the hard bits, with none of the windows of lightness that occurred in the calm. 'She really is fine, Ben.'

'It doesn't sound as if she's fine.'

'Tammy,' Misty called through the door.

Tammy's voice came back, softly, a little spaced with the focus of her thoughts on the baby inside her. 'Yes?'

'Tell your father you're OK, please, honey.'

'I'm fine, Dad.' Then the next contraction came and she began to moan.

Ben wrung his hands. 'I don't think I can stand this.'

'Go for a short walk, Ben. I'll phone your mobile when she's ready. I need to get back in with her.' She shook her head and kissed his cheek. 'I can't believe this. You've seen hundreds of babies born and you're a mess.'

Half an hour later Ben heard the words he barely dared to hope for.

Tammy's voice. 'I want my dad!'

Misty opened the door and Ben swept past her and knelt beside the bath to hold his daughter's hand. As he gazed into the sweat-beaded face of the young girl he'd watched grow into this powerful young woman, he thanked God and Misty, the woman who had saved him in more ways than one, so he could be there for his daughter at this moment.

Suddenly, it was all over before Ben had even realised how close it was, and Tammy's baby was born.

'It's a boy,' Tammy said softly and lifted her son from the water to cuddle him against her breasts. 'Hello, there, little Jack.' She looked at Misty and Emma and then at her father as if to say, See what I've done.

'I'm going to call him Jack because I've always liked that name for a boy. Then, of course, he will be Benjamin after his grandfather.'

'Jack Benjamin is a lovely name,' Ben said, and he shook his head at the glowing woman that was his daughter. 'I'm so proud of you, Tammy,' he said.

She looked serene and proud of herself, too, and he owed a lot of that to Misty for having faith in his daughter he hadn't had.

He looked across at his wife and blew her a kiss. He dared to hope she'd forgiven him for taking his stress out on her. Again.

'Congratulations, Grandpa.' Misty smiled and the love in her eyes promised bucketfuls of forgiveness, and a life of love and laughter and wonderful times that he'd only ever dreamed was possible.

FREE

2 BOOKS AND A SURPRISE GIFT!

We would like to take this opportunity to thank you for reading this Mills & Boon® book by offering you the chance to take TWO more specially selected titles from the Medical™ series absolutely FREE! We're also making this offer to introduce you to the benefits of the Mills & Boon® Book Club™ —

- ★ **FREE home delivery**
- ★ **FREE gifts and competitions**
- ★ **FREE monthly Newsletter**
- ★ **Books available before they're in the shops**
- ★ **Exclusive Mills & Boon Book Club offers**

Accepting these FREE books and gift places you under no obligation to buy; you may cancel at any time, even after receiving your free shipment. Simply complete your details below and return the entire page to the address below. You don't even need a stamp!

YES! Please send me 2 free Medical books and a surprise gift. I understand that unless you hear from me, I will receive 4 superb new titles every month for just £2.99 each, postage and packing free. I am under no obligation to purchase any books and may cancel my subscription at any time. The free books and gift will be mine to keep in any case.

M9ZEE

Ms/Mrs/Miss/Mr.....................................Initials ....
                                                                    BLOCK CAPITALS PLEASE
Surname ....
Address ....

....

....Postcode ....

Send this whole page to:

The Mills & Boon Book Club, FREEPOST CN81, Croydon, CR9 3WZ